For Freedom, For Glc

This edition ©James Morfa Churchill 2024
First Published in 2017

This is a work of fiction and whilst real people have been used they are in no way representative of their real life counterparts.

-CHAPTER I-

As I stepped out onto the jetty I was struck by an overwhelming stench of shit from the Thames. In London this is no trifle, especially as the city keeps a manure type odour for the majority of the time. This is especially true of days in late August when the sun is angry and her heat becomes so unbearable that a gentleman has to undo his collar to prevent his shirt from clinging to him with a nauseating glue of grime and sweat. Had I visited the dock beforehand I would not have chosen it as a place to receive a royal princess. I would not have accepted the word of my housekeeper's husband that it was as good a place as any other. Then again, I supposed, if this was to be her first whiff of the great imperial power-house then the remainder of the city, for however brief a time the princess spent here, would smell like a lavender meadow by comparison.

At the same time as arriving at the end of the jetty I saw the steamer which carried my princess approaching from down river, from the direction of Deptford. No glorious or stately pleasure craft. A working barge, dirtied and worn almost to scrap by years of carrying coal. Its name was *The*

Coxcomb[1] and for the price of three guineas I had been able to have my princess brought, discretely, into the city from the luxurious surrounds of her yacht, moored off the Isle of Thanet.[2]

Secrecy and discretion were vital to the enterprise. She was in grave peril. There were men, fanatical men, revolutionaries, pursuing her, and they wanted nothing more than to see her head removed from her body. These men had dogged her across half of Europe, first catching up to her in Venice, chasing her through the Italian lakes into Switzerland and then up through France and to Paris where my own people had finally taken her in hand.[3] We arranged for her yacht, which had been somewhere in the Baltic, to be brought to Calais from where the princess was then shipped across the channel.

Even here, in England, she was far from danger. The revolutionaries would have known that she was bound

---

[1] The Coxcomb was built in 1839 by Mason & Brigitte, shipbuilders of Rotherhithe. It carried coal, and later wool, along the river until 1893 when it was sold and broken up for scrap. At the time of these events it was owned by a man called John Morgan.

[2] Specifically, it was moored within the shelter of a small headland east of Margate. Its name was Ankerwinde, which translates into English as 'Windlass.'

[3] By 'my own people,' Max refers to the secret agents of the Morfasson family business. At that time the business was called NITIDUS.

across the channel and they would have sent word to their local allies to watch for signs of the yacht.

I had made sure that there was little chance she would be caught by them. As soon as the yacht was within sight of England I had the steamer dispatched to Thanet and the princess brought along the Thames to this foul smelling dock on the Isle of Dogs, suggested by my housekeeper's husband.[4]

Before the steamer had moored, as it was approaching from down river, I saw *her* standing proud on the prow, large nose high in the air and a haughty expression worn her face. Her beauty did not strike me, but she was by no means foul. Her eyes were what first caught my attention; they were brown and betrayed a bewitching wickedness that I could not help but take to my heart. I could not see her hair at this stage, it was covered by a bonnet, but it was of the same brown colour as her eyes and naturally curly. Her mouth was rather large and her lips crossed much of her face. What my mother would call a fish mouth. The fact that those lips were pursed and turned downwards made her appear quite frightening.

---

[4] Framlingham Gil, a dockyard inspector.

The steamer moored and the gangplank lowered, she moved from her position at the prow and as fast as she could she barged her way onto the jetty, brutally knocking the crew of the steamer aside with no consideration for where they might end up.

I saw that she had defied my most important instruction and was wearing an expensive and highly fashionable summer gown.[5] Highly inappropriate given the situation. It made her appear as she was; classy and well to do. It made her stand out. If the revolutionaries were nearby, which was always a possibility, they would know her in a moment.

Something would have to be done about that. I could not take her through the streets of London looking like *that*.

'Miss Anna,' I doffed my hat as she tried to push past me and she gave me a silent, unamused expression. 'I am sorry to ask this, but do you, by any chance, have any clothes that might be somewhat less… ostentatious?' The expression on her face said that I had offended her.

'No I certainly do not. I cannot be seen to walk around in

---

[5] Telegram transcripts indicate that the staff aboard the yacht were instructed to dress 'the princess' in clothes that would make her appear inconspicuous. The diaries of her chief maid, Frau Grubel, reveal that when told of this she balked and stubbornly refused to wear anything besides her own clothes.

the clothes of common washer women. It would be highly undignified.'

'Undignified it may be, but it is a necessity if we are to prevent the revolutionaries from discovering your whereabouts.' The princess harrumphed a great deal before, with much protest on her part and few words from myself, she surrendered.

'Very well. Do *you* have any low born clothes which I might wear?'

Ah! Therein lay a problem.

I had considered that she would have brought her own clothes, that she would have been sensible enough to follow my instructions and disguise herself from the revolutionaries.

'I gots some you'm might 'ave miss,' the steamship captain cried from the gangplank. 'My daughter Ginny, she done goes leave a spare clothes set on here for when she goes to visit her aunt in Canvey. They be not as glam'rous as your current garb but they's quite pretty all the same.' The princess, I thought I heard, growled. She disapproved but she had little choice if she wished to deflect the gaze of the revolutionaries.

She retired up the gangplank and a considerable time later returned, her previous attire folded underneath one arm. Now dressed in a passable but old and faded white cotton dress that was hardly big enough to fit her. As she came back down the gangplank, once more knocking the crewmen out of her way, she looked more sour and haughty than she had done previously.

She thrust her discarded gown into my grasp and folded her arms.

'I do hope,' she said, 'that you shall be taking me somewhere I shall not need to dress in this hideous fashion.'

'Of course,' I said. 'I shall be taking you to my family home. The revolutionaries will not, or should I say *hopefully not*, find you there.'[6]

'Will there be society? High society I mean?'

'At the present moment in time. When the season ends, however, there shall be considerably less.'

'I see. You shall be taking me somewhere else at that point.'

'It depends on developments concerning these

---

[6] The village of Cythry (in some annals referred to as 'Caer Cythry) was then in the county of Carnarvonshire but is today part of the county of Conwy, though only just.

revolutionaries. We shall have to see when the time approaches.'

'THAT was not a matter for debate. You SHALL take me somewhere else. Now what of the climate? Is it agreeable?'

'When I left three weeks ago, almost certainly. But the weather in those parts can change in a heartbeat. Today it could be bright and wondrous sunshine but tomorrow it could be blowing a tempest the likes of which you have never seen in your entire life.'

'It sounds dreadfully ghastly,' she grimaced. 'At least tell me it does not smell so foul as here!'

'No. It does not. The odour is far more agreeable.'

'And what of my retinue?'[7]

'They shall not be joining us for the moment,' I said. 'When the threat of the revolutionaries has passed, perhaps then.'

'Do you have servants of your own?'

'Some. I do not have as many as other households. At present there is only myself to attend.'

'I see. Well... The sooner we get there the sooner we may

---

[7] Anna's retinue had been left aboard the yacht as a means of fooling the revolutionaries into thinking she was still aboard. How this rouse was received by the revolutionaries is unknown.

arrange the place to my satisfaction.'

She began to frogmarch me down the jetty, hooking my arm into hers as though we were promenading along the pier at Llandudno.

At the end we came to the dockyard, full of workers loading and unloading and checking cargo. The princess looked to be quite afraid of them and almost stopped dead but kept moving when she saw that they were paying us no heed. As far as they were concerned I was no more than a gentleman escorting his lady friend from the steamer that had just moored. They would never know that she was a princess, not even from the crew of the steamer who had all promised on the bible that they would each be the soul of discretion.[8]

On the road out by the front of the docks our hansom cab was waiting. It was, in actuality, a private vehicle made up to *look* like a hansom cab. This was once again all for the protection of the princess. The driver, who was of course dressed to look like the driver of a hansom cab to complete

---

[8] The owner of the dock, in his diary for that day, wrote that rumours were abounding amongst the men that a 'well born lady' had passed through and they had been told this by none other than the steamship captain, John Morgan. The owner dismissed the rumour as poppycock.

the illusion, was stood by, awaiting us. and he doffed his cloth cap as we approached. He was my regular driver, my chauffeur if you will, and he was a dear man by the name of Codswallop.[9] Short and plump with a long grey beard, he looked rather like something you might see in a children's fairy-tale picture book.

'Afternoon sir. Afternoon miss... You'll be wanting Euston station I presume? Grand! Grand! It'll be tuppence ha'penny if that suits sir, miss.' He opened the door to the cab and stood aside to allow us entrance. Bowing

'I am a *highness*, not a miss,' the princess corrected him rudely. It was my job to correct her.

'Unfortunately, Miss Anna, that cannot be allowed. We must keep your station under wraps. Even when we reach my home we must keep up the illusion that you are a miss and not a highness.' The princess was much aggrieved and made huffing noises as we entered the cab.

Codswallop seated himself ahind the horses and with a great 'gee up' myself and my princess found ourselves rattling along the cobblestones of London and away from

---

[9] His full name was Anthony Cecil Johannes Codswallop. His family were said to have been the carriage drivers to the Morfas family for twenty generations before him and he was the last of his line.

that foul smelling dockyard.

-CHAPTER II-

I cannot, I suppose, keep referring to her as 'the princess.' I should tell you who she was and where she came from. Her full title was 'Her Royal Highness the Princess Anna Von Carrolus of Ardeluta'[10] but as a matter of convenience I shall hereby refer to her as Anna. Ardeluta, her kingdom, or principality as it should correctly be termed,[11] was one of those small, insignificant European states that one hears vague mention of from time to time but has no clue where they are.[12] It is a tiny enclave completely surrounded by Romania and it is comprised of one small town, a single village and the royal palace. Having never been there myself I cannot describe it to you in my own words so you will instead have to rely on second hand testimony.[13]

Ardeluta is a mountainous area, full of forests which climb

---

[10] Some sources claim her title to have been 'Serene Highness' rather than 'Royal Highness' but this appears to be a mistake.

[11] Anna's diaries, and those of her chief maid, always use the term 'kingdom' over 'principality.' Principality is the correct term.

[12] It lies in the north west of modern day Romania, about 105 miles west of the border with Moldova.

[13] Much of this testimony appears to have been lifted from Anna's personal diaries.

to the top of high slopes and block out the shape of the escarpments beneath. Within these forests you will discover the usual glades, babbling brooks and cave systems, each with a story or legend attached. Much like Wales. It is a land of mystery and magic, a land where the people are deeply suspicious and well set in their traditions and ways. Again, much like Wales.

Being remote Ardeluta is, quite naturally, untame. All kinds of creatures roam the countryside. For example, wolves and the sounds of their howlings can be heard on many winter nights. It is small wonder, as a result, that the people of these parts talk of werewolves and do not dare set foot outside after dark.

There are bears here also, not the great brown grizzly ones of Alaska and Canada, which I have seen with my own eyes, but the smaller, darker, European variety. They are no less deadly than the more ferocious grizzly. I have heard Anna tell of groups of children who went off into the woods to play and only one chap returning, crying of bears snatching his fellows away in their jaws.

Of the town, it is called Tarcau. Humble. no larger than somewhere we ourselves would call a village. There is a mill and a trader, several traders in fact, and somewhere the young are educated, though not a school as such. It has no architectural merit. All of its buildings are plain and most typical of the surrounding area. The village meanwhile, after which the principality is named, is of only a few houses and hardly worth mentioning.

The palace is said to be a marvel.[14] It is built in the style of an Italian renaissance villa, resting on the plateau of a mountain which overlooks the village. All the trees about it have been cleared so that the building can be seen from a great distance, a statement declaring the supreme authority of the Crown Prince of Ardeluta, who at this time was Anna's father, Prince Gustaff.

Down the mountainside before it lies a series of sweeping terraces and gardens. Each was elaborately planted, full of well trimmed hedges and so perfectly manicured that it takes no less than twenty gardeners to maintain. On a central terrace is a great fountain that squirts its load to twenty feet over the mountainside[15] (so I am told) and comes down

---

[14] Its name was The Athelstein Summer Palace and today no trace of it remains above ground. Archaeologists can't seem to find it underground either.

[15] Most sources say it was only seven foot, which seems more likely.

again in a magnificent, thundering cascade.

Opulence was[16] the key word when it came to matters concerning the interior. Not one room was humble or decorated in a quiet style. All was gold or silver or exquisite marble and each room was covered from floor to ceiling in frescoes, art works and paintings by the great Italian masters; Canolleti and Titian and Bartolenni. The ballroom was the grandest of them all, measuring the same length as the nave of York Minster.[17] It was not so high as there but from its ceiling, which was entirely covered with gold leaf, hung five huge chandeliers of the finest crystal cut glass. On each wall were one hundred mirrors so the dancers could see themselves dancing to the strains of music from the royal orchestra, music which filled the room from one end to the other. It was, in a word, a very ostentatious and over the top sort of place.[18]

Despite all this extravagance and expense the royal family were only in residence during the months of June and July.

---

[16] Max changes tense here. It is recorded that the palace, though it remained standing for a period of years, was stripped of furnishings and ornament by members of SHEMBLE immediately following the revolution.
[17] This would make it around 249 feet long.
[18] No wonder the locals were cheesed off!

They spent the remainder of the year flighting about the fashionable resorts of Europe. They spent April and May in Italy and in August they could always be found with the Grimaldi of Monaco, swanning about the Mediterranean and hosting banquets aboard their sailing yachts. In September they would decamp to the Baltic, to the Swedish archipelago and to Copenhagen, before working their way down through France and Switzerland to their private winter resort in the Alps.[19]

The family were not of Romanian origin. They could claim direct descent from the first Crown Prince of Ardeluta, Titus, but this was through a female line and the Von Carrolus dynasty were of Austrian descent. My readings would have me believe that they inherited the title upon the death of Prince Amreich in the year 1730. Their dynasty had never accustomed themselves to the Ardelutian people or their way of life and they had wasted no time in spending all the limited crown revenues and raising up magnificent debts, for which they had to squeeze their subjects to the last penny.

---

[19] This was called the Piz Von Carrolus and it was somewhere near to Klosters

Anna's father, Prince Gustaff, was more frugal than his predecessors. He at least understood what the crown could and could not afford to spend. Early in his reign he settled the acquired debts by the personal fortune he had acquired through marriage[20] and as a result he was able to ease the financial pressures upon his people.

However, the damage had already been done by the actions of his predecessors. The Ardelutians were bitter and resentful towards their rulers after a century and a half of extortionate taxation, a bitterness not helped by the fact that the royal family were only ever in the principality for a little less than two months of the year.

As tensions are ripe to do this one had snapped the previous summer when the royal family were in attendance.[21] With the backing and support of a wicked mercenary organisation by the name of SHEMBLE, the local populace stormed the palace, planning to overthrow the royal family. Word had already reached the family of this coup and the night before the storming they had fled the

---

[20] His wife was Gloriana di Ravenna, daughter of an Italian noble.
[21] The final straw was, allegedly, the striking of a local farmer by Prince Carlo, Anna's brother and heir to the principality. The veracity of this act is unknown.

palace, never to return.

Bitterness grew, especially amongst those who felt they had been wronged on a personal level, and this led to the formation of a fanatic militia, a group whose sole aim was to track down all the members of the royal family and dispense justice in the name of the people. Again they had the backing of SHEMBLE and thanks to their influence other fanatics from outside the principality joined them. Although they totalled less than fifty people, they very nearly succeeded in obliterating many of the Von Carrolus family.

All of them had managed to find safety with the exception of Anna, whose luck had been short. As I described in my previous chapter, they had dogged her across Europe. How they knew where she would go I have not the foggiest. It was not, I am certain, any member of her retinue as upon their arrival in Paris my men had thoroughly investigated each of them and all were clean. It was, I suppose, pure ill luck.

Seeing no other way out it had been decided, by Prince Gustaff no less, that Anna should be given over to my protection until the revolutionaries, as he himself named them, had returned home in defeat. How long that would be nobody could say but I knew of only one place in all of Europe where a princess might possibly hide from revolutionaries her whole life and never once be found- My home in North Wales, Cythry.

-CHAPTER III-

Anna was transfixed by London. She had seen cities before, I know. She had seen all of the other capitals of Europe. None of them though can ever hope to compare to that which lies at the heart of the British Empire, and not in any good way. Paris is a beauty and Rome is ancient and grand but London is a brute. It is vast, sprawling out in all directions so that if you were to walk from one side to the other it would take you no less than a week.[22] Ninety percent of the place is not pretty. It has buildings of architectural merit, certainly, but these are outnumbered ten to one by slums and filthy old hovels.[23] It is a place blackened by soot and smog and smoke and cutting right through its heart are the dirty brown waters of the Thames, which is not a grand or stately river by any means.

London is an ugly city.

From those docks on the Isle of Dogs we passed through the slums of the east end, perhaps the ugliest part of that

---

[22] He's clearly exaggerating. Couple of days at most.
[23] Max knew the slums well, having lived for much of that spring in the Westminster slum known as The Devil's Acre.

ugly city, with its run down houses and all the people shuffling by in their ragged clothes which had been in the possession of half a dozen others before them.

Over the rattling of the carriage wheels on the cobblestones we could hear their cries and conversations, their guttural calls to one another, and when she first heard their voices Anna pulled a funny face.

'Their language… It is not pretty,' she said, covering her ears before continuing to stare out of the window at all these people whose language she thought was 'not pretty.'

When we reached the square mile, merging into the slow moving traffic, Anna removed her hands from over her ears and was more pleased. The buildings were still not meritorious, they never shall be in London, but at least now they were backed by the splendid dome of St Paul's, which Anna approved of. She said that it had 'an aura about it.' The people too were more to her taste. They were gentleman bankers, stock brokers and investment traders in pressed suits and bowler hats with gentlemanly moustaches and beards. Alongside were well to do women in white satins, wielding white parasols to shield themselves from the white hot sun. They were mixed in with the poorer classes too but the rich overwhelmed them by a great many.

'I like these people better than the ones we saw before,' Anna said.

Movement towards Euston was tedious and our conversation was light, limited to Anna's likes and dislikes regarding the buildings and people she could see from the window.

Out of the square mile we kept on the direct path to Euston, passing up Fleet Street where the throngs were so mixed that were it not for their clothes it would have been difficult to divulge who belonged to which class. Anna quite disapproved of this intermingling. In her view the poor, and she expressed this fiercely, should stay within their own circles and never mix with the higher classes. She was, needless to say, much happier when we turned into Belgravia and the crowds became more exclusively higher class, though not entirely.

We reached Euston at the top of Woburn place and once again, as we stepped down from the carriage, Anna expressed distaste that lower classes were mixed amongst well to do society. She said that there was no acceptable situation where the classes should mix in such a fashion. I ignored her and made a show of paying Codswallop his cab fare.

Codswallop doffed his cap and climbed back into his seat before driving away, and I took Anna by the arm.

'Please remember to keep your voice down, at least here. We cannot allow the slightest hint who you might be. You must appear as an ordinary member of society.'

Anna gave a loud harumph before allowing me to escort her into the station.

Our train, the *North Wales Express*, was waiting at the third platform. Anna protested as we passed the first class carriages but my warning about her appearing as an ordinary member of society soon curtailed her.

I next felt her shudder as we reached the third class and again as I opened a door and then for one final, third time, once we were inside.

'I presume we will not be aboard this choo-choo for long?' I enjoyed the way she called the train as a 'choo-choo.'

'We shall be spending the night aboard. Arriving at some time tomorrow morning.' Anna's eyes flashed like fire before she daintily placed herself in one corner.

'Why is it that for such a small island your trains are so

dashed slow?'

'I do not know, Miss Anna.'

'We are alone,' she snapped. 'When we are alone you must refer to me as *Your Highness*.'

'No. It is best we get into the practice of being on more equal terms even when alone. We must keep up the illusion that you are ordinary at *all* times.'

'I hate this illusion.'

'You may well hate it, Miss Anna, but what is the alternative? Your life?'

Anna folded herself further into the corner and put on a petulant frown. Clearly she did not hate the illusion so much that she was willing to risk her life in spite of it.

'If I am to be Miss Anna then what, pray tell, am I to call you?'

'Max shall do. Some would sniff at the familiarity but…'

'It is necessary to keep up the illusion!' Anna proceeded to laugh, the first time I heard her do so. It was a girlish, throaty thing that rang melodically in the ears. 'What would I call you if we were being less familiar?'

'Mr Morfasson,' I said.

'Mr More-Faz-Un?' she attempted to repeat phonetically.[24] I shook my head.

'Not quite. More-Fur-Sun... As in the sun in the sun in the sky.' Anna tried again.

'More-Fur-Sun... More-Fur-Sun...' After a few more tries she got it. 'Morfasson... It is a peculiar English name.'

'It isn't English. It's a Danish-Welsh hybrid adopted by my distant ancestors. Morfa is the Welsh word for marsh. The Danish part is the son at the end. It comes from the old Viking patronymic system... So it technically means 'Son of the Marsh.'[25] I don't think Anna understood a word of my explanation but she still gave a polite nod.

'Tell me,' Anna ejaculated after two or three more minutes of discourse, 'is there a Mrs Morfasson?'

'No. Nor any potential candidates at the present moment.'

'Ah well. At least you are a man. You have many years left to find a wife. A woman, according to society, must marry young. My father, he is always pestering me on this. He says

---

[24]Will, James and I got sick of instances (like this) where people couldn't pronounce our last name- I've had Morf-ASS-on. Morrison, Monsoon and Morph's Sun- The solution was to shorten it to Morfa.
[25] The origin of the name Morfasson is actually a matter of debate. That which Max describes here is only one theory.

to me: Anna, we must find you a suitable husband, quick sharp! At the present I do not feel that I would like a husband though.'

'Would you ever?'

'Perhaps. If the right gentleman were to propose marriage I might accept.'

'I *was* engaged once,' I told briskly. Anna's eyes glowed with delight.

'Oh really? What became of your betrothed, if you don't mind my asking?'

'She died... Cholera, in Dublin nine years ago. Daphenia was always a sensitive soul and when she heard of an outbreak, in Dublin, she rushed over there to attend to the sick. She ended up catching it herself, poor lamb.' A sense of melancholia swept over me and I had the peculiar urge to continue telling Anna of Daphenia.[26] It was not the time nor her place to know those things, however, so I reserved myself.

'What of yourself Miss Anna? Have you ever been tempted by the call of Eros?'

---

[26] Daphenia Brooke, of Dublin. She was the daughter of a brewing magnate but not much else is known of her.

'No I have *not*,' she said crisply.[27] I took her at her word.

Before we had a chance to talk further we found ourselves interrupted by the arrival of three buxom ladies.

'I'm sure these folk won't mind if we share their cabin. Do you mind?' They were northern.

'No. We do not mind,' I smiled. Anna's look of fright as the three sploodled into the compartment was humourful and she pulled herself yet further into the corner as the largest of the women meteored down right next to her, almost on her lap. The remaining two ladies sat either side of myself. I was hardly able to breathe for want of space.

'Ooh, I do like to sit next to a handsome gentleman on the train. Don't you Mabel?' That was the lady to the right of me and her voice was high pitched.

'I do Maureen… I do! And this one is *certainly* handsome.' That was the lady to my left and she grabbed my arm in order to pull me closer to her. I struggled to get away and Anna found my discomfort amusing.

'Well I don't mind so long as we get to swap round later

---

[27] Anna may have been lying in her response to this question. Francois Del Firenze claimed, in a work published in Italian in 1934, to have spent a romantic summer with 'a princess of Ardeluta' at some point during the 1870s.

Max & Anna

on,' the lady on the opposite side threw in. 'So long as his lady friend here doesn't mind.' Anna pursed her lips and pulled herself upright.

'You may take him away if you so wish it,' she preened. 'You may do with him whatever you will and I would care not a jot.' The three ladies began to cackle at each other.

'Offended her have we?' one of them jested down my ear. 'What did you do then? Did you say something coarse to her?'

'He has done a great many things to offend me,' Anna said. 'But that is not why I say you may take him. He is merely my escort and we are not a lady and a gentleman in any romantic way.' The three ladies all made 'ooh' noises towards each other.

'What she says is quite correct. I am her solicitor, Mr Clapham. I was assigned by her father to escort her to the house of her cousin in the north.'

'His name is Friedrich,' Anna suggested without being prompted, which I was pleased about. 'He is a merchant seaman.'[28]

---

[28] Anna did indeed have a cousin called Friedrich, although he was not a merchant seaman. He was an illegitimate son of Count Rhineskeller.

'My brother is a seaman,' Mabel announced. 'Solomon Mufty. He sails out of Liverpool.[29] Does your cousin live there too?' This was rather a presumptive statement, I thought. There are more ports in the north than Liverpool. Anna, whose British geography was not strong, looked to me for guidance.

'No.' I answered for her in a hasty fashion. 'He is of Caergybi and does much of his merchant trade with Dublin.' The women again made their 'ooh' noises towards each other.

One of them pressed close to Anna. It was Mabel. This appeared an intimidating thing to do, especially as she was seated on the opposite side of the compartment.

'You're not from around these parts are you my dear?' Anna frowned with confusion.

'I do not understand what you mean.' Her tone was acidic.

'I mean you're from foreign climes aren't you?' Anna gave her a withering, gorgon's gaze.

'I am indeed.' She turned that gorgon's gaze upon myself.

---

[29] Another, more peculiar tome in our archives gives mention of a sailor called Mufty who 'blew his boat up last winter.' Unknown if they are the same- See: *Red Bird*.

'Mr Max,' she said aloud and in front of the three ladies, 'Perhaps you and I should walk down the choo-choo until we come to a quieter compartment.' The ladies, at the suggestion, all made melodramatic moans and waved their arms in the air.

'Oh it's like that is it?' Maureen cried. 'It's considerable rude, that's what it is. You invite three amicable ladies to share your compartment and then decide you wish to go elsewhere!'

'No no… You misunderstand,' I jumped in. 'It is nothing of the sort. Miss Eustacia suffers from migrainous headaches and we did not expect the three of you, pleasant as you are, to be so voluble.' The three ladies remained in stunned silence for a moment. Then they began to talk again.

'Oh, we'll be quieter, won't we ladies?'

'Oh yes. We will, we will,' all three chittered in the manner of birds.

'I am sorry Miss Eustacia,' the woman next to Anna cowed. 'We didn't mean to be so inconsiderate.'

'That is quite forgiven,' Anna said.

And then there was silence. The train whistle blew, a piercing shriek, and we all found ourselves chugging out of

Euston and along the tracks that would take us, eventually, to Wales. That was all the noise there was for a long time, besides the rhythm of the train of course. But the silence which reigned from then on was an awkward, unnatural, forced one. The three ladies were not used to being silent amongst one another. They were used to chittering and wittering away as though there were nothing more important or necessary in the entire world. They desperately wanted to chitter and every so often it would seem that one of them was about to say something but then thought better of it. before continuing to remain silent.

You could have cut into the atmosphere in that compartment with any kind of instrument, even the bluntest of blunt ones. The tension caused by the silence was unbearable. Even Anna, for whose insistence it had come about, looked uncomfortable by it.

It could not last and after the first ten minutes had passed I began to think that it would break at any moment. It took far longer than I suspected it would at the time, at least an hour more, before it happened.

'Oh I can't stand the strain any more Arrabella,' Mabel cried, standing up and placing her hand to her forehead. 'I must talk... I must tell you about Mrs Dominic and that blasted cat of hers... It's always in the outhouse so it is. You want to go in and do your business and there it is perched on the seat and it won't budge for Jesus or the end of days!' When she finished this babbling, though why she had wished to babble on the subject of Mrs Dominic's outhouse pussy only heaven knows, she flopped back down to the seat, exhausted. The remainder of us stared in bewilderment and it was Anna who broke the ice.

'Have you tried glass bottles filled with water? I have heard that the creatures see the reflection of their own eyes and think it is a rival.' Mabel looked upon her in a considerable way.

'You know Miss Eustacia, I have not heard of that one before and I've tried all sorts. You name it I've tried it. I've thrown a bucket of ice cold water over the thing but all the wretched beast did was howl.'

'Not all cats hate water. I had one when I was a little girl,' Anna said. 'She was called Stasia and she used to *love* the water. Every morning I would place her in a bowl of water and splash her and rub her all over and never once did she protest as people always suppose cats do.'

'Well what a curious thing. To tell you the truth Miss Eustacia I have never taken to cats. I have always had more of a preference for dogs.'

'Pah… Dogs!' Anna scalded. 'Dogs are for hunting and nothing more. Keep them as a pet and they become needy creatures, always wanting one thing or another. Not like a cat. A cat will look to its own devices and it shall hardly ask its human co-habitants for anything.'

Again, after Anna had finished speaking, there was silence. This time it was not so much of an awkward silence but a comfortable, congenial one without the unbearable tensions. It did not last nearly so long either, only a matter of minutes over the previous, strenuous hour. This time, instead of it being one of the women, it was Anna who broke the silence.

'Mr Max, do you by any chance have any reading material about your person?' I gave her a look of sheer addlement and then one of complete and total embarrassment. I had not, suffice to say, brought reading material for either of us.

'I do apologise Miss Eustacia,' I said. 'But when I sent our luggage ahead I appear to have placed your reading materials within, quite without thinking I am afraid.' Anna scowled and growled at me.

'Then perhaps you could go and find me some. There will be a library aboard the choo-choo somewhere, yes?' Maureen let out a belly laugh.

'A library aboard a train! Whoever heard of such a silly thing?'

'Where I come from all choo-choo have a small library aboard,' Anna said. 'Perhaps, Mr Max,' she turned back to myself at this point. 'Perhaps, Mr Max you might go and see if you can find me either a library or some reading material.'

'And leave you by yourself Miss Eustacia?' She brushed me away.

'Do stop fretting Mr Max. I shall be perfectly fine to do without you for a few moments.' The smile she gave me was curious to say the least. Nevertheless, I fell to believing her and relieved myself from between Maureen and Mabel in order to find Anna some reading material. It would do no harm, I supposed.

I wandered down the coach as far as the guard's van in order to make enquiries but the guard was quick to inform me that there was not so much as a book aboard, not for lending at any rate. He did however suggest that I might find someone with a newspaper willing to pass it over as soon as they were done reading it. This I found three compartments along from our own, in the possession of an elderly gentleman who was dressed in his best tweed and cloth cap. He promised that he would pass the newspaper down to my compartment when he had done so. I thanked him for his kindness and returned to the compartment in order to tell Anna the good news.

Were it that simple. I had been gone for only a few minutes and in that time she had fled the compartment where once more the three ladies were chittering away like birds.

'Oh, she went to look for you,' Arrabella told me. 'She said you were taking an awfully long time.' I soon developed a suspicion as to where she had fled and immediately set out in the direction of first class.

Sure enough that is where I found her, in the first class dining lounge with a glass of red wine in her hand and a huge smile on her face. She was still dressed in the clothes given to her by the steamer captain and looked quite out of place amongst the chintz and the fine furnishings of first class.

'Mr Max… I was wondering when you would find me. I hope you do not mind but I have upgraded our tickets.' I was struck dumb by her statement. 'I promised the conductor that you would pay him when you arrived.'

'We should really be in third class,' I insisted. 'The revolutionaries would not expect to find us there.'

'My dear Mr Max, that, if they are aboard this choo-choo, is precisely where *they* will be. They are not the sort who would purchase a first class ticket for, how would you English say it? Love nor money!'

'But if on the slight chance they *are* aboard this train they will come here to look for you. They may not look in the third class.'

'So let them look. What could they do to me aboard a choo-choo? There is no escape, there are many guards and if they *do* happen to locate me then we shall depart at the next stop.' I thought this to be a rather naïve view of things.

'That is besides the point Miss Anna. I would rather not have them locate you *at all*.'

'Well we shall just have to take the risk shan't we. I could not abide sitting near those women for a moment longer anyhow. They were so vulgar. As I said to you earlier, Mr

Max, the classes should not mix. No matter how I am dressed or the fact that I am hiding from these revolutionaries I am still a high born lady and I should not have to mingle with riff-raff.' I was set to respond but she held up her hand to silence me. 'And I do not care for your illusion Mr Max. I shall wear these clothes with sufferance and I shall pretend that I am ordinary but I shall *not* mingle with riff-raff. There must be a limit to the illusion and that is very much beyond it.'

I sighed, concluding that there was to be no arguing with her. If she was set upon remaining in first class then that is where she would remain, no matter my strongest objections.

'Well then,' I announced. 'If we are to remain here in first class you cannot stay wearing those rags.' Anna beamed and from underneath her derriere she produced the glamorous dress she had been wearing when she first alighted from the steamer.

'Then I shall change back into this… Just as soon as I have finished my wine of course.'

-CHAPTER IV-

It was to be a sleepless night. I first paid the conductor for our upgraded ticket which resulted in a higher price than that which I would normally pay, owing to the fact that I was upgrading *after* we had set foot aboard the train and a considerable way into the journey. This left me seething but that was not to be the reason I was to have a sleepless night.

Anna's snobbery regarding the lower classes meant that she was now in a situation where she might be discovered by the revolutionaries. She had set my plans awry and now I needed to compensate. I had to keep a watchful eye out for revolutionaries for if they were to strike then they would strike in the night when we were most likely to be off our guard. Therefore I absolutely *could not* sleep as I had to act as the guardian angel, watching over Anna in her slumber.

I lay awake on my bunk, listening, and once or twice I prowled out into the corridor to check if anyone were lurking, to see if anyone suspicious were searching the compartments for signs of the princess. In all I found no one nor saw any signs of any lurkers but that wasn't to say I could let my guard down. I had to be alert at all times. The revolutionaries could have struck at any moment and I had to be prepared to defend Anna at all costs, to give my life for hers if it came down to it.

The previous day I had sent a telegraph to Cythry and ordered Belvedere[30], my butler, to greet us at the station in Aber[31] with three horses. At a little before half past eight we arrived. Earlier, grouchy from my lack of sleep, I awoke Anna and told her to once more dress in the steamer captain's clothes. Once this was done, with a deal of protestation, I escorted her back to third class where I found a compartment, empty, from where we could depart the train. Despite Anna being insistent on exposing herself to the revolutionaries I could still take steps, such as these, in order to confound them. They would expect someone of her stature to leave from a first class carriage and so we would depart from a third. If on the small chance they knew we were aboard *and* in first class then they might, with luck, assume we had not yet alighted.

---

[30] John Belvedere, born in Nasareth, had been butler to the Morfasson family since 1853.
[31] This refers to the station at Abergwyngregyn, which closed in 1960.

We were the only pair to leave at Aber station and so hurried away before any of the other passengers could take notice of us.

The sun was shining that day, a blessed day as we call it in Wales, and although Belvedere had not yet arrived it was a pleasure to wait for him. Anna wanted to wait by the sea shore and so we did just that. I pointed her towards the various sights that could be seen about Bae Conwy. To the east, Pen Y Gogarth and to the west Ynys Seiriol, a tear drop on the end of Ynys Mon. Immediately across the water I picked out Beaumaris and the castle, to which Anna laughed.

'You call that a castle? It is quaint and teensy. A true castle is big and imposing. A true castle is grand.' I said nothing on the matter, hoping to surprise her once we reached Cythry.

In due course Belvedere arrived, strolling down the road with three horses in tow, an open necked shirt on his back, and a straw boater upon his head. He looked ridiculous.

'You are the butler?' Anna questioned him right off.

'I am indeed. And you must be Miss Anna.' He bowed, ever so lightly and delicately. 'I can tell that you are wondering why I am dressed in this fashion. It is not my usual attire. I merely considered that it might serve to confound the revolutionaries in a manner similar to that of your own dress.'

Ah, such was Belvedere. He was always considering but never thinking and as a result he was usually getting things in a muddle. This was not his absolute worst faux-pas, not by a long chalk, but it was still off the tracks somewhat.

'Belvedere,' I said to him, sounding exhausted, 'you are extraordinarily well known in these parts. Dressed in that fashion people will start talking and gossiping, wondering why you are wearing such a get up. Now imagine if the revolutionaries got wind of that gossip. Why, they will ask, is the butler to the most famous family hereabouts dressed in such a fashion? They will start to think and then they may leap to the not so wild conclusion that the reason involves a certain princess.' Belvedere looked agape as he realized his folly and began to make profuse apologies. 'Save it Belvedere.' I ordered. 'What is done is done. We should proceed to Cythry as planned.'

Belvedere held out one of the horses for Anna; a chestnut colt who was friendly to strangers and without a fiery temperament of any kind. She climbed onto his back precisely as you would expect from one who has been riding horses all her life. I was then handed one of the remaining horses, my favourite. Like the other he was a chestnut colt but he could not have been more different from his fellow equine. I was the only person he would allow to sit upon his back and even then he showed signs of resenting it. My orders were obeyed with a lingering hesitation and more often than not I had to tell him twice before he would even begin to think about what I wanted him to do. Secretly, I think he enjoyed our rides together. His eyes would always light up as I saddled him and his tail would begin to swish as that of a dog. His gait became visibly more jolly too and his head always rose that little bit higher, as though he were proud to carry me. I loved that horse more than I have loved any before or since. No longer do I own *any* horse owing to the advent of the motor car but even if I did no beast could replace that chestnut colt in my affections.[32]

The three of us aboard our steeds, Belvedere turned to me.

---

[32] Max first bought an automobile in 1899, a Peugeot type 16, and he bought two more cars (An Oldsmobile 'Curved dash' and a Corbin) before he sold the last horse owned by the Morfasson family in 1905. Over the century that followed the family car collection grew at an astonishing rate and today it includes some two hundred of the best and worst examples of automotive history.

'By which route shall we ride home sir?'

'Which way did you come from?'

'Through the Eigiau pass sir... And then along the Roman road that runs besides Drum.'

'Then we shall return by the more direct route across the high plains. Perhaps, Miss Anna, you would like to see the magnificent Aber falls along the way?'

'Yes indeed. I would like that a great deal.'

And so we set off at a brisk trot back towards the station and then down the secluded lanes of Aber village that would eventually lead us to the falls. I hear rumour that once there was a palace here, belonging to the royal house of Aberffraw, though where it actually was I could not tell you for the life of me.[33] It was also somewhere in these parts that Dafydd, the last true prince of Wales, was captured by the forces of Edward Longshanks, ending the last days of an independent Wales. By the way he was attempting to flee, into the mountains, he was probably attempting to reach

---

[33] The location of this palace is a matter of some debate. Some suggest it was in the centre of the village where the remains of a high status building have been discovered, resembling a winged medieval hall. Others, meanwhile, suggest that it is the nearby manor house of Pen-Y Bryn, to the east of the village.

Max & Anna

Cythry.[34] Had he reached there and not been captured on the slopes of Bera Mawr his fate would likely have been a similar one. My ancestors had played the war for both sides, on the sly, and as a result they were allowed to keep all their lands and titles, unlike many other members of the Welsh aristocracy of the time.

These facts I told to Anna as we passed through the village on our way to the falls. The part she seemed most interested in was that concerning my ancestors being 'Welsh aristocracy.'

'So you are Lord Morfasson, yes?' she beamed.

'Not exactly. By the time the Glyndwr rebellion happened in fourteen hundred it was well known that my ancestors had played both sides during the conquest. Glyndwr, when he was crowned, stripped us of our titles as punishment. King Henry did the same, as well as confiscating most of our lands, in order to make sure that we wouldn't be able to side with Glyndwr.'

'Who did your family side with?'

'Both sides. We were split. Some supported Henry, others

---

[34] Max gets this detail wrong. Dafydd wasn't fleeing. He was actually in hiding at a mountain farmstead by the name of Nanhysglain.

Glyndwr. The ones who supported Glyndwr were executed and Henry gave back the lands to the ones who had supported his cause as payment for loyalty. Not the titles though I am afraid. After that we learned to steer clear of internal political conflicts. By the time of the civil war in the seventeenth century we were just content to cash in on the chaos. Us and the Blackadders.'

'These lands you talk of, you still retain them?'

'Some. They are not so large as they once were. We retain the ancestral seat and the nearby village. That is about all.'

'Would your Queen Victoria give you a title?'

'Not bloody likely. My father insulted the memory of her beloved Albert. It was not I who did it and yet she still holds me to what my father did.'[35]

'Then my father shall give you a title for protecting me. You shall be Lord Morfasson of Ardeluta!'

'If it is all the same Miss Anna, I would rather be paid with money than with a title.'

It was not long before we left the village and were passing

---

[35] He, also called Albert, point blank refused to donate money towards a local memorial to Prince Albert upon the death of the latter in 1861. His reasons for this refusal are not known.

along the tree lined avenue that leads to the falls. We caught no glimpse of them until we rounded a sudden kink in the road.

They were just the same as they ever were and just the same as they ever will be; thundering downwards in a ribbon from the high plains; a great rush of water that pounds down a rugged cliff face and returns to the earth with a sound so loud that one can barely hear oneself speak above it, even from a fair distance. At the time I could therefore not ask Anna her opinion of the falls for this reason, although I saw that her face was a picture of indifference.

'It is quaint,' she would tell me later on. 'Much like that castle across the sea.' When I told her that it was the largest natural waterfall in Wales she laughed and said that if that were the largest then the others could hardly be considered waterfalls at all.

We pressed on, having observed the falls, up into the mountains by way of a track that is used by tourists to reach the top. There, after scaling a further small rise, we found ourselves on the high plains of the Carneddau mountains, the craggy grey of Bera Mawr looming before us and the rounded gnoll of Llwytmor on our left.

Our pace quickened, the wind almost blowing our hats from off our heads, and we raced towards Bera Mawr, rounding it to the right so that we might eventually come to the peak of Bera Bach, then again turning left so that we had seen Bera Mawr across three sides. As we reached Bera Bach we stopped and looked towards Bethesda. The nearest mountain across the valley was blackened and cut open, belching ugly clouds of smoke into the sky.[36] It looked like the entrance into hell.

'Who would dare do such a terrible thing to this lovely place?' Anna asked, horrified.

'The Baron Penrhyn,' I sneered before turning my back to that heinous monstrosity.

The sight was forgotten as we set our horses cantering southwards across the plain, towards Yr Aryg and Garnedd Uchaf.[37] In places the ground was rough and rocky and here we had to proceed slowly. In between Uchaf and Foel Grach, where there is grassland Anna decided that she

---

[36] This mountain is called Carnedd Y Filiast.
[37] Although still unofficially known as Garnedd Uchaf, this mountain was renamed Carnedd Gwenlian in 2009.

would throw caution to the wind and as she rode undid her bonnet from about her head and allowed it to fly away to somewhere it would never be found. The look of ecstasy upon her face said more than words ever could. She was happy, grateful to be alive and have the wind in her face and the mountains about her.

She came to a stop on the far side of Foel Grach, seeing a group of wild ponies charging across the valley below. Again, the look of joy upon her face said more than words ever could.

'Mr Max, you never told me that you had horses near to your home!'

'Aye… But they aren't the best part,' I laughed.

'Oh? And what is the best part?'

'Follow me and I will show you!'

I began to trot away across the valley before breaking into a gallop, Anna coming close behind and Belvedere a distant third. I lost my hat as I hit the slopes of Llewellyn but hang it, I had plenty more. The going became rocky here so I had to slow but not by much. I turned east before I reached the peak, heading downwards, and found myself on a sharp track. Then it was around one more bend and home was in sight. I stopped before it, as I knew Anna would when she rounded the bend behind me.

She came to a halt in a clattering of hooves and whinnies and nearly fell from her horse in her astonishment.

Father always said that the single best way to impress any woman, be she princess or commoner, was to show them Cythry.[38] His words never rang truer than on that day as Anna looked down for the first time in awestruck admiration at the many turreted, sweeping and enormous castle before her. It took her breath away, and no wonder. No other castle in all the world comes as close to majesty and beauty as Cythry does, even in a state so ruinous as I have always known it.[39] Anna said but four words in all the time we stared at it.

'I am in love!'

---

[38] I can fully endorse this statement. It works with guys as well.
[39] In 1880 the castle appeared much as it does today, with only the keep and the kitchen block remaining standing. The only major difference is that a small part of the upper keep was destroyed in 1963.

-CHAPTER V-

We rode down the remainder of the mountain to Cythry with Anna in a dream state all the way. Had I not known the castle my entire life and had I never before set eyes upon its glory I would have been quite as enraptured as she was at that moment. You cannot imagine, dear reader, unless you have borne witness to that structure, how awe inspiring it is. I would encourage you if ever you are in the area to make a detour and gaze upon my home for yourself.[40] It is not marked on any map but you shall have no trouble finding it if you follow the side road off the highway between Capel Curig and Llyn Ogwen.

Outside the entrance we left our horses with Belvedere who promptly departed to return them to their stables down at the edge of the village. Anna was keen to see the interior of Cythry and so without waiting she ran to the doors, flung them open and stepped, astounded, into the marble floored entrance hall. She flung her arms wide and span around like

---

[40] Please be aware that CCTV is in operation and monitored 24/7. Anyone wandering beyond the designated right of way is liable to prosecution.

a ballerina, her eyes filled with twinkling delight. She ran to the sitting room on the left and then the drawing room on the right before nosing into the dining room and shrieking at the muralled ceiling.[41] I stood at the foot of the stairs, awaiting the conclusion of her self guided tour, and by the time she returned she had been rendered speechless.

'Would you care for some tea Miss Anna?' I asked, going towards the drawing room.

'No. Thank you Mr Max. What I would like instead is something which I may eat.' That sounded quite the idea to myself also. It made me realize how hungry I was. I rang the service bell and Constance, one of the young maids, appeared in double quick time.[42]

'Ah... Constance...' I began but was interrupted by Anna.

'Girl... I would like a grapefruit.'

'I'm afraid we don't have any grapefruit miss,' Constance blushed apologetically.

'Then what fruit *do* you have?'

'We've got strawberries and gooseberries miss. I think we

---

[41] The mural depicts the Battle of Camlann and was painted by Raphael Scottari in 1705.

[42] Constance Ashbury. Born C.1860. Yorkshire. She worked at Cythry from 1874 to around 1890. Little else is known of her life.

may also have some plum chutney in the pantry.'

'Then I will have the plum chutney spread thickly onto some toasted bread. And a glass of sparkling water if you have any.' Constance curtseyed to these whims.

'I'll have a large slice of ham, Constance. Perhaps wrapped around some pickle? And do we still have any of that delicious cheese? Cachu Geifr? I'll have some of that as well. And we'll eat in here.' Constance curtseyed and left to prepare our food whilst Anna looked about her, befuddled.

'Mr Max, how can we eat in here if there is no table? Or do you plan to be decadent and uncouth?'

'Decadent and uncouth is indeed my plan,' I defended. 'I find there is something quite liberating about not eating at table.'

'It is obscene,' Anna protested. 'It is not dignified. Refined and civilized peoples do not eat wherever they happen to place themselves. They do not eat like *that*, in the manner of common road menders.'

'So you would much prefer to dine at table?'

'Indeed I would Mr Max. Indeed I shall. Whilst I am resident in your house so shall you. If we are to share company then I shall see to it that you behave in a civilized manner.'

So when Constance returned I informed her of the change of plan and we ate in the dining room. It seemed like such a waste to me. I, normally, only used the dining room on formal occasions. The remainder of the time I ate in either the drawing room or down in the old servant's hall. I could see Anna balking at eating in the servant's hall and so I did not make the suggestion to her, despite the fact that it was no longer, strictly speaking, a functioning servant's hall. It had to be the dining room for I sensed that nothing else would suffice.

Our food eaten in ridiculous ostentation, I escorted Anna to where she might find some clothes more suited to her taste. In her delight at the magnificence of Cythry she had quite forgotten about the rags she was wearing and when I suggested she change she suddenly remembered and jumped at the chance.

'Why yes, I *must* change. I absolutely *must* be out of these rags at once,' she shouted.

Thankfully my home has an entire room dedicated to spare clothes and cast-offs where someone might find something to wear for any occasion. Quite often my father would bring friends up from London and he would insist that they travel as lightly as was possible and that they make full use of this room. Upon every shelf was a dress or suit, sometimes faded, or perhaps a summer gown. There were bathing costumes and sports clothes and things for hunting or riding in. It was also the most likely place where Belvedere acquired his earlier get up as there was, tucked onto a top shelf, a selection of similar garb.

Anna insisted that she and I go through the entire room, picking out all the clothes that she might wear for the duration of her stay. We ended up with three piles. If Anna liked something enough to think that she might wear it then that item of clothing, whether it be a gown or a dress or a coat, found its way to the first, neat pile by the door. If she liked something but not nearly enough to wear it then she would make a passing comment before placing it on another neat pile. The third pile was the largest and least neat. These were the clothes Anna loathed and she cast things aside onto this pile with gay abandon. A lot of them, I noted, were my mother's clothes[43] and I was most put out when she threw a

---

[43] Max's mother was Lavinia Morfasson, nee Cartwright. She was the well-to-do daughter of a celebrated Bedfordshire jockey.

yellow ball gown of hers onto the pile. I always loved that gown and Mother had looked beautiful in it. To see it flagrantly tossed aside broke my heart.

'What on earth is *THIS*?' Anna asked, pulling out a large white dress covered with huge jewels and excessive amounts of padding. I ran a finger over it.

'It is Tudor, I believe,' I told.

'Tudor? My dear Mr Max, no modern lady would wear a Tudor dress. This belongs in a museum!'[44]

'I think there might be a Tudor gentleman's outfit around here somewhere. Yes… Here we are…' I found it next to where the dress had been. It was brown with golden trims and equally excessive padding. Anna laughed at it.

'Tell me… Would you wear that Mr Max?'

'Perhaps if it were a parade or something of the like,' I admitted. Anna laughed and shook her head.

'No Mr Max. That is not good for wearing in any circumstance. Dispose of it Mr Max. That and anything else which is not modern.'

The search for clothing concluded, I showed Anna to a

---

[44] In actual fact, the dress IS now in the basement of Bangor's *Storiel* Museum, although the jewels have been replaced by paste imitations.

Max & Anna

bedroom where she could change and later sleep and repose. She hated it. Her reasoning was that it was too small and dark and so she set off, myself and the pile of acceptable clothing close behind, to find a better room. She put her nose through every door but she did not find a room which she liked until she came to the top of the castle and discovered one opposite to the library. This was large enough and with enough light but there was still one issue; a picture of my estranged sister Mable upon one wall. Declaring the room would be acceptable without it, I left Anna to change and deposited the picture facing the wall of the library. I cared not to look at the thing which is why I kept it in a room I never used.

Five minutes later, unexpectedly, I saw Constance come running down the hallway and enter Anna's room. She did not leave and five minutes later the second maid, Sophia, came running down the hallway and entered Anna's room.[45] I wondered, stupidly, what on earth might be going on before I realized that they would be assisting Anna in trying

---

[45] Sophia Brackett- Born April 1849. She left service to be married to a Bethesdan cobbler one year after these events and died during childbirth five years following.

on the dresses and gowns. Having only known her to dress herself for the previous day I had grown accustomed to the idea that this was usual practice. I had forgotten that she was normally dressed by an army of servants. Now that she had them again, or the use of them, she was taking full advantage. I wondered, for a deluded instant, what her reaction would be if I were to dismiss the entire staff (all four of them) so that we were left to our own devices, but brushed it away as a silly idea. Anna would only go and hire an entire entourage of people in their place, I considered.

After a long interval, during which I answered my correspondences in the library, the three women emerged from the room, each bright and cheerful. Constance was carrying a small pile of the dresses across her arms.

'See that you perform those alterations at the earliest convenience,' Anna ordered. Constance curtseyed to her.

'Yes Miss Anna. Is that all Miss Anna?' It was, for the moment, and the two maids hurried away to their duties.

'I like your servants,' Anna announced as she entered the library and looked about her. 'They are very obedient. They are very loyal.'

'That is my late mother's doing. She wouldn't hear of

hiring lacklustre staff. She always used to say to me: Max dear boy, always hire the best. Never settle or you will always rue the day.'

'She was correct. Even one poor servant results in a poor household.'

'I have always stuck to her advice and I have never once regretted it. Not like the Earl of Beddgelert. He's always hiring poor staff and he's always having to replace them.'

'Who is this Earl of Beddgelert? Is he a man of high standing?'[46]

'Oh yes. Very high. Yourself and his lady wife would get on very well I feel.'

'Then I should like to meet her. At the earliest possible convenience.'

'That should not be a problem provided we keep your status secret. How does tomorrow sound? I can have Belvedere telegraph him right away if you so wish.' Anna jumped and clapped her hands.

'Oh yes. I should like that very much. Does he live far?'

'Beyond Yr Wyddfa.'

---

[46] In 1880 the Earl of Beddgelert was the 5th, Sir Avebury Cadbury-Cavendish.

'Yr Wyddfa?'

'Yes. It is a mountain. A large one.'

Anna went to the window and looked about at the scenery.

'Can it be seen from here?'

'Not from here no. There are too many other mountains in the way. We could perhaps walk to where we might see it later on, if you like.'

'That would be most admirable Mr Max.

She remained gazing through the window for some time whilst I continued with my correspondence. When I had finished I stood behind her and we both looked out upon the same scenery. About us were the Carneddau mountains, Llewellyn and Daffyd most prominently, and below us the placid waters of Llyn Cythry.

There was one feature which I did not notice until Anna pointed him out to me. He was a man, dressed in light linen threads and holding a wooden staff in his left hand. He stood, with a skill that few could manage, on an exposed and precipitous crag of Llewellyn, looking right towards the castle.

'He has been there for some time,' Anna worried.

'Yes. He's a high hill farmer. Call themselves Frodorion.

They're sort of like the Scottish highland clansmen and keep to themselves mostly. He probably saw us riding across the mountains earlier. He'll have recognized myself and Belvedere and he's probably curious about yourself.' Anna pulled away from the window and took shelter behind the wall.

'Then send him away. I do not like him being curious about me.'

I did not know what to say. Clearly she was frightened by the curiosity of this man. I knew without having to look twice that he was Frodorion, I knew him personally to a small degree, and I knew he would be no harm whatsoever. He lived as part of an isolated farm group and would know little, if anything, of the world beyond the Conwy river. He would certainly not know of the revolutionaries and would not be any part of them.

Seeing her reaction to this man told me one thing concerning Anna. Underneath her haughtiness and her snobbery, underneath her desire to remain as respectable as was possible, she was frightened. She was frightened of the revolutionaries and what they might do to her and even the curiosity of a lone stranger, who really meant no harm, was enough to send her into a panic.

-CHAPTER VI-

The man on the mountainside shook Anna something terrible. When we dined together that evening she confessed that his presence *had* reminded her of the revolutionaries, reminded her that they *could* be watching her wherever she went. I reassured her that she would be safe in Cythry but it did little good. That night she slept but two hours at the most. She awoke at every noise the old castle made, every rattle of the windows and every creek of the floorboards. Somewhere in the eaves of the attic space above her lived a nest of owls and the fluttering of their wings as they came and went made her fear that someone could be lurking in the roof space, waiting to leap down and strike her dead.

Needless to say she was in no mood to see anyone the next morning. I had a telegram sent to Beddgelert informing him that we would not be visiting that day as Anna was 'unwell.' A reply was prompt and it said that we should come as soon as we were able. I spoke to Anna of this and she readily agreed, implying that if she could sleep for the next two nights then the visit could be undertaken.

For this I ordained to do the best I could. I first had Belvedere knock up a draft of his mother's magic sleeping elixir. That stuff was a wonder. You felt nothing for an hour and then all of a sudden you were out like a light.[47] Absolutely bloody marvellous! I don't know what went into it but if I did I would almost certainly give you the recipe.

The second thing I did was move Anna away from the owls and to a room where they would not disturb her. Of course, she protested. She protested to the heavens that the room I placed her in was too dark, it was not, and that it was too small. In fact it was bigger than the entire living space of most working class families. To this fact she played the princess card, declaring that the working classes were *supposed* to be confined to small spaces but that people of *her* class deserved to be somewhere large enough to befit their stature. She gave up eventually, finding that I would not back down on this matter, but for the remainder of the day I would not here the end of how I was maltreating her.

Towards noon I was in my office, attending to some paperwork, when Belvedere knocked upon the door. He was

---

[47] We found the recipe and unfortunately it turns out that old Ma Belvedere had invented Rohypnol one hundred and fifty years early.

extremely prompt in declaring his business.

'Sir. There is a Frodorion man in the drawing room. He wishes to speak to you.' I jumped up in alarm, worried that Anna might see him and recognise him as the same sort of man as was stood on the mountainside the day before. I considered that it may frighten her all the more to see him *inside* the castle.

'Where's Anna?'

'In the library sir. The last I knew she was rearranging the books. Apparently they were in an ungodly order.'

'Good.' I hurried to the door. 'Keep her in the library. Do not let her leave until I have dealt with this Frodorion.'

Down to the entrance hall I raced, wondering why on earth this man, who came from a people who rarely spoke to folk from outside their own communities, should want to speak to me. It was exceedingly rarer to see one enter the home or business of someone from what they call 'the outside.'

They are, the Frodorion, a generally untrusting people. They do not like strangers and they are not fond of anybody who attempts to become overly friendly with them. They see this as suspicious and assume that an individual is being friendly not because he wishes to be but because he is out to

James Morfa

exploit them.

This will come as little surprise when you learn of how they have been treated by outsiders in the past. They do not keep records, relying instead on oral traditions, and they tell that after the Edwardian conquest of 1282 the English soldiers treated the hill farmers with far more severity than they did the rest of the native population. Their settlements were ransacked, invaded in the Frodor dialect, and their children taken away and their women raped. In more recent times the settlements have again been ransacked, though by a different menace to the medieval English soldier. I refer here to industry. In order to obtain the wealth beneath their soils dishonourable men came without warning and destroyed their farms in order to dig huge pits and mines. The Penrhyn quarry at Bethesda, the Dinorwig near Llanberis and the quarries around Blaenau Ffestiniog were all dug at the site of Frodorion villages. This issue of destruction has become so prevalent that there are now almost no major hill famrs south of Dyffryn Ogwen. All of them, with the exception of one close to Moel Siabod above Capel Curig and one in Nant Ffrancon, are located within the bosom of the Carneddau mountains. There is one, for example, on the slopes of Cwm Eigiau and another not far from Llyn Dulyn.

Throughout our many years occupying the lands the farmers and my family have developed a begrudging respect for one another. We are not friends, one can never truly be friends with a Frodorion farmer, but we are amicable towards one another. They know we will do them no harm, nor bother them in any great manner and we respect their traditions and customs, which is more than can be said for most. Many would see them scorned and cast asunder as immoral and ungodly, 'unchristian' I suppose you might say. This is despite the fact that they *are* actually a Christian community. They know my family to understand the landscape and the mountains and because we show care for the land and do not disturb the delicate balances of nature by digging out the hillsides for profit they respect us. They consider themselves to be a part of that balance. Without them, they claim, the mountains will crumble and the seas shall reclaim all the lands of Eryri.[48]

---

[48] It is interesting to note that during the first half of the twentieth century, thanks to improved technology, many Frodorion farmers began to mix with the rest of society and as a result most of their traditions and customs were lost. As a distinct group they have all but disappeared. As

This Frodorion who broke with custom and entered my home I knew personally. He was an old man of at least eighty years of age, though as his people do not keep records I cannot be more precise than that. His name was Gyddyn and he was head of the Dulyn village.

I found him in the drawing room, staring out of the window with a pout and a look of concern in his amber eyes.[49] I approached and bowed my head to him. He nodded back to show his acceptance of my greeting. Had he been any man other than a Frodorion we would have shaken hands but the Frodorion do not like to be touched. For them only a wedded couple or a suckling mother and babe may touch one another. To touch in other circumstances is considered a great offence.

'I shall come to the point, Faban-Morfa,'[50] he said abruptly, in the Frodor dialect. 'This lady whom you brought across the mountains yesterday. Who is she?'

'She is a client,' I answered truthfully in the same dialect. 'I

---

yet the mountains have not crumbled, nor has the sea reclaimed the land.
[49]Reports say that most Frodorion farmers had amber eyes, probably as a result of inbreeding.
[50] Their name for all members the Morfasson family. It means 'Marsh Child.'

have brought her here to safeguard her from men who wish to see her dead.'

'But who *is* she?' Gyddyn demanded. I grew immediately concerned as to why he was so interested in knowing who she was. I had brought strangers to the castle before, many of them, and never once had the Frodorion shown an interest in them. They knew of these visitors, I know. I know because we had seen *them* as we walked through the mountains, watching us from atop the peaks and gnolls.

'May I ask why you are so interested in her?'

'She is stained by blood. She is red from foot to head.'

'How do you mean?' I puzzled.

'The old women have seen her in their dreams. She brings death and danger to these mountains. She brings death to my people and to yours. Who is she? Who are the men who try to kill her?'

He was not a man to go spilling secrets. I could trust him. His culture would never allow him or give him the opportunity to reveal anything to the revolutionaries so I could inform him of everything. I told him who she was, that she was a princess of Ardeluta. Then I had to explain where this was by aid of an atlas. Then I explained of the revolution and of how the populace had turned against the royal family and the reasons why.

'Her family are wicked for betraying their people, but their people are worse for turning upon their leaders,' Gyddyn philosophized.

'I assure you that she is not a bad person. The doings of her family are no fault of hers.'

'We are *all* responsible for the behaviour of our ancestors, especially those who can no longer be responsible for themselves. This princess shares the burden for the betrayal of her people.'

'That doesn't mean she deserves to die,' I shot back at him, trying not to demonstrate any anger.

'No. It does not. In that we agree. As I said, the men who hound her are worse. Any man who kills in cruelty is a more evil man than one who lives from the exploitation of others. If it were *my* business the punishment of the princess would be to live with the guilt of forging these more evil men. Live with the knowledge that the blood on their hands is her doing.'

Gyddyn paused and turned back to the window.

'These men will come here. Even this fortress is not safe.'

'How can you be so sure? I took a great many precautions in bringing her here!'

'They will come. Just as the old women have seen her stained by blood they have also seen the men. They *will* find her.'

Most, including myself, would dismiss this as claptrap but the Frodorion are a highly superstitious group. They see all dreams as being prophetic. The older one gets the more powerful these prophecies become and the dreams of old women are seen as the most important and powerful of all. I thus did not dare speak out. It would have been rude and disrespectful for one thing and for another I was aware that it was entirely possible that these men would somehow find her, that they *would* come to Cythry. It was not likely, Cythry was isolated enough and unknown enough that even if they tracked her as far as Dyffryn Ogwen they would not likely stumble upon the castle. I would still have rather that did not happen however. The further away they were the better.

'I shall heed your advice,' I told Gyddyn amicably. 'I shall make preparations for their possible coming and in the event they *do* come I shall ensure there is as little bloodshed as possible.'

'Beware of this princess Faban-Morfa. She brings the blood to this land and I fear we shall all rue her presence.'

His warning given, Gyddyn departed and left me to reflect upon what had been said.

-CHAPTER VII-

I showed Anna as much of my homeland as I could over the following three days. By the evening of the same day as my meeting with Gyddyn she was once more feeling her usual self, having slumbered in a library chair for much of the afternoon. After dinner she expressed a desire to take a stroll about the village and I was only too happy to oblige. The evening looked to be a bounteous one, the sunlight glowing red off the mountains and giving the village a warm, continental feel. If I had told Anna then, and she did not know we were in Wales, that this were an Spanish mountain town in summer she may well have believed me.

At around seven we set out from the castle and strolled down the cart track towards the village. The first building we came to was a crofter's cottage and the crofter (who was called Jones) was in a chair by the side of the road, smoking a long white pipe. He lifted it from his mouth and saluted us with it.

'Bore da,' he greeted in an old, raspy tone. I repaid the greeting by doffing my cap and answering in kind.

'What is bore da?' Anna questioned once we had gone by.

'It is Cymraeg. The native language of Wales. It means good day.'[51]

'Can you teach me more of this Cymraeg?'

'Of course. Bore da is a formal greeting so if one wanted to greet someone less formally one might say: 'Iawn cariad,' although I must add that this is usually more of a working class greeting and someone of your class would likely not use it. It means hello my love.

I demonstrated with the next person who passed by, a lady with a basket walking towards the crofter's cottage. She smiled at me and responded with a simple 'iawn.'

'And how would I introduce myself?' Anna delighted in discovering this.

'Very simply. You would start with a bore da, always a bore da if it is someone you do not know, and then you would say your name followed by 'dwi.' So in my case I would say 'bore da, Max dwi.' In your case you would say 'Anna dwi' after the bore da.'

'I always thought you English to be so formal. I always thought you never used forenames.'

---

[51] It is only in Cythry where 'Bore Da' is used to mean good day. It actually means good morning. Good day is 'Dydd Da.'

'That is true, in England, but this is Wales. The varieties of surnames here are few which makes such formalities impractical.'

'And if two people have the same forename? A common one such as John? What then?'

'They would still most likely use their forename, at first, but where a name is especially common, where there are many John Jones for example, they are known by their trade. A cobbler called John Jones might be known as Jones the shoe for example.' Anna roared with laughter and clapped her hands.

'Oh that is so marvellous. You should export that around the world. Every country should name their people with names like 'Jones the shoe.' It would not do for high born people of course. Their names would be all the same. They would all be names such as Von Spitzburg the duke. But for the lower classes you should certainly export it.'

We continued to walk down the track to the village and its short rows of slate roofed, centuries old cottages. The people who live here are poor but under the stewardship of my family they are assured of all they ever want. So long as they pay their rents at the end of each month their gardens and cottages will be maintained, tended, and kept well furnished. They are never given reason to complain. If there comes a time when a man cannot pay his rents then we have always been most understanding. We do not expressly demand the money from them but we endeavour to learn why they have not paid. If that person is suffering through financial difficulties or going through a personal trauma then they have our assistance, advice and generosity. If, however, they are missing their payments for a reason that is more selfish and unscrupulous, and in the past a select few have tried it, we are not so kind. We take a hard line on these people and they are given a notice of one month, after which they must vacate their cottage. It has never been difficult to find replacement tenants as people know that life under a Morfasson landlord is one of the best and most beneficial in the region.

Anna stopped our walk in the centre of the village where all of its three roads came together. On one corner of this junction rests the *Oak and Crozier* tavern, which Anna pointed to.

'Mr Max,' she cried. 'I have heard of the old English inn. May we see inside?'

'It is not an old English inn,' I reminded her. 'This is a Welsh tavern. A much rougher sort of place.'

'But may we still see inside Mr Max? I would like to see what such places are like.' I hesitated and she continued to beg.

'You are aware that many, perhaps all, of the people in there are of the lower class? As you have stated yourself, the classes should not mix.' Anna humphed and pursed her lips.

'We do not need to mix with them. We shall arrange for a table to ourselves.'

Before I could say that there might not *be* a table, it is only a small place barely large enough to fit half the village, she was marching for the door and barging her way inside. There were but four patrons at that stage of the evening, plus Rhonda the barman,[52] and all were talking loudly.

As the door opened and they set eyes upon the newcomer their reaction was typical of the type any stranger might receive when entering a local Welsh tavern. They fell immediately silent and eyed her with a great suspicion, locking on their gazes and preparing to interrogate her as

---
[52] His full name was Aneurin Bryn Rhonda, though he was only ever known as Rhonda.

she stepped towards the bar. They only eased when they saw me hurrying in behind her. If she was with me, they must have thought, than her presence in their domain was tolerable.

'Iawn Morfas,' Rhonda greeted as we approached the bar. 'Got yourself a new lady friend then?' We spoke to one another in Welsh but I have here rendered our words into English for the ease of all my readers.

'Oh no. Nothing of the sort. She is here for her health. Her father suggested that the Welsh mountain air would do her the world of good.' Rhonda nodded and held his hand towards Anna.

'Evening miss. My name is Rhonda and it is my pleasure.' Anna pinched his hand with her fingers in a regal sort of way. It was *too* regal for my liking.

'So you are known as Rhonda the beer, yes?' Rhonda frowned.

'No miss. Just Rhonda. What has Morfas here been telling you?'

'I have been explaining Welsh surnames to her. 'Jones the shoe' and the like.

'Ah.' Rhonda beamed. 'That's only for people with

common surnames. Rhonda isn't that common so I'm just plain old Rhonda. John Evans over yonder though,' he pointed to a man across the room. 'He's known as Evans the horse on account of the fact that there's another John Evans in the village. He's Evans the horse because he runs the stables and the other is Evans the cut.'

'And what does Evans the cut do?'

'Not much anymore Miss. Not since he can no longer work. But in the past he worked as a slate cutter up at Bethesda.'

'Poor bugger lost the use of his hands in an accident and got kicked out of the quarry. I took him in and now he acts as my assessor, seeing how much cottage repairs and such things lwill cost.'

Anna gave an amicable sign of approval before looking around the room and eventually coming back to Rhonda.

'I shall have a pint,' she declared. Rhonda and I stared at her.

'Are you sure miss?' It's just that the ladies who come in here don't usually drink pints. They drink gin usually. Or I got some wine back here if you'd prefer?'

'No. I shall have the pint. I am told that it is something one must try.' Rhonda squinted at her.

'Where'd you hear that miss? I don't know anyone who'd suggest that a British pint is worth a try.'

'I am from Austria. It is a common saying there,' Anna answered plainly before turning to me. 'Mr Max. Shall we seat ourselves in the corner by the window?' It was a pleasant spot she suggested, perhaps the most pleasant spot in the tavern, and so I agreed.

The pint was pulled, well… two pints were pulled considering I ordered one for myself, but before we could retire to our seats Evans the horse came to the bar and made a suggestion.

'Perhaps you'd like one of them names for yourself miss… Like Jones the shoe? What do they call you?" I thought, from the look on her face that she might answer with 'her royal highness' but she did not.

'They call me Miss Anna.' Evans the horse had a short thought and then laughed.

'Why then, we'll have you known as Miss Anna the pint. How does that sound?' Anna snorted and laughed so loud that I had to hold her upright.

'Yes. You may know me as Miss Anna the pint… Provided

you give Mr Max a name also.'

'He's already got a name Miss Anna. He's known as Morfas the thief.'

'Because he steals your livelihoods and monies?'

'No. Nothing like that coz he don't. He's a fair and just landlord so he is.'

'They call me Morfas the thief,' I began to reveal, 'Because when I was a scrap of a boy some chums and I broke into the Penrhyn slate Quarry and stole three cartloads of cut slate.'

'That is deplorable!'

'Maybe so but the Baron Penrhyn ain't no friend to this village. He deserved the kick in the teeth Morfas and his chums gave him. We roofed the whole village on the slate that he brought back.'

'Aye. We did. But I'm not proud of what happened next. Penrhyn blamed his own workers and had twelve of them transported to Australia for theft.'

'It is not fair to blame someone when you have no evidence against them,' Anna said.

'They had evidence against them alright Miss Anna. They planted some slates in their homes and said that they were the ones that went missing.'

'The more I hear of this Baron Penrhyn the more I begin to dislike him. He does not sound like a good leader for this land. He mistreats the people and accuses them of theft, works them in a hellish looking mine, and if Mr Max is to believed he never spends any time here.'

Put in that way the Penrhyns sounded awfully similar to the ruling family of Ardeluta. They too were absentee rulers who mistreated their people and I wondered if Anna saw the same similarity.

'He sounds as though he deserves as many kickings as can be given.'

'I agree Miss Anna… But you can only kick a man so many times before he notices and kicks back.'

'Leave it with me. I shall consider a novel way in which we may kick him.'

'Please do not do anything rash Miss Anna,' I begged as we finally retired to our corner.

'Rash Mr Max? I shall do nothing of the sort. What I shall do will be carefully considered.' I let the matter drop and hoped that by morning she would have forgotten her idea to kick the Penrhyns.

She tried her pint, gingerly at first, and for the first quarter or so she was not certain that she liked the taste. But continue to drink she did and eventually she came to love it, soon expressing a desire for a second. She even went to the bar and ordered it for herself. It was my money that paid for it, naturally, and whilst she was at the bar Anna spent a great deal of time talking to Evans the horse and one of the other four punters, Benedd. What they talked about I do not know. She returned, second pint sloshing over onto her hand, extremely happy.

As she was drinking that second pint the tavern filled up in double quick time and at a guess I would have said a whole two thirds of the village were crammed into the tiny room.

Movement was hardly possible and people had to come, much to Anna's alarm, and sit down next to us. They gave us a bore da and we returned the favour, Anna being fairly timid in her delivery. It didn't take long for her to grow used to them and she soon became enormously comfortable around them, even being so happy as to briefly converse with a lady, Emmeline Jones, about why she was drinking a pint.

There not long after came a point where she started to ask

me about who people were and what they did. I was happy to oblige her. The only thing that appeared to truly disgruntle her was that much of the conversation amongst our fellow tavern dwellers was in Welsh and she could not eavesdrop on them.

There was a stage in the evening where she attempted to drag me into eavesdropping by proxy but that was not a good idea. The other punters may have been speaking Welsh but they could speak English just as fluently and they would know what we were up to.

At the close of the second pint a tall man entered the tavern and whilst nobody else batted an eyelid at him Anna gave a voluble shriek of surprise. He noticed and kept a large brown eye upon her as he ordered a pint from Rhonda. He began to make his way over and Anna clung to my arm for protection, though she needed none.

'Mr Rhonda tells me they're calling you Miss Anna the pint,' he smiled at her. 'I'm a foreigner here myself, even though I've lived in this land for getting on near sixty years now.' He held out his hand for her and she gave it a regal pinch.

'How did you find yourself here in Wales?' Anna asked

him, attempting polity despite an obvious trepidation.

'By what other means? Slavery! I was born on a plantation in Jamaica and sold to the Penrhyns when I was five…'

'They owned slaves?' Anna looked at me, horrified. 'Slavery was an awful thing. They are truly abhorrent people.'

'Aye. That they are Miss Anna the pint but it is not only the fact that they owned slaves which makes them abhorrent, bad as that were. An awful large proportion of the British establishment owned slaves… The Prime Minister, Mr Gladstone, his father had plantations and he was not so much of a wicked man as Penrhyn. By many it was seen as normal.'

'Did the Morfasson own slaves?'

'No we did not,' I spat back in disgust.

'So I am presuming the Penrhyns brought you here to Wales?' Anna pushed.

'That they did. I worked on their Jamaica plantation for fifteen years, being flogged, beaten and shackled. I still have the scars even sixty years later.' He placed his arms on the table and rolled his sleeves up to reveal hideous looking marks about his wrists and up his arm. Anna reeled back in horror and I looked away. 'After fifteen years they decided they didn't want me on their plantation and had me shipped over here to Wales... When they abolished slavery...'

'Which they fought against,' I added.

'Which they fought against! I was left with nothing. I was thrown out on my ear but Mr Albert took me in and gave me a home and a job and I've been here ever since.'

'He was a grand man was Mr Albert,' someone shouted in Welsh, followed by a chorus of 'Aye.'

'And do you have a name?' Anna asked, ignoring the interlude of praise for my father due to a lack of understanding.

'I'm so sorry Miss Anna the pint. Did I not mention it?'

'No you did not.' She folded her arms very crossly and he laughed.

'You brought a mighty fine woman to the village this time around Mr Morfas,' he laughed. Then he held his hand out to her once more.

'John Douglas. Solicitor to the Morfasson family.' Anna let out another shriek of surprise. He grinned at her. 'Quite a climb up from slavery, I agree. Mr Albert paid for it all. He spent years educating me, teaching me to read and write, and then he put me into the temple bar and made me into a solicitor.'

'He was a grand man was Mr Albert,' someone repeated followed by the same chorus of 'ayes.'

'And what did you give Mr Albert in return?'

'Eternal gratitude, a friendship that lasted to the day he died. I taught his children how to sing!' He said this last part with a wicked glee, like he knew it would prompt Anna to ask me to sing. When she indeed did this I promised I would do so when we were out of the public gaze. My tenor was rusty.

There *was* singing that night, though it did not come from myself. It was started by a drunken Benedd who began a Welsh language variant of Molly Malone[53] and this soon descended into a cacophony of local folk songs from across the ages. One of them, the song of Ceilliau the dragon, involved someone dancing at the centre of a circle and people were dragged from their seats to take part.[54] I refused to fall into this revelry and so they took Anna instead. She

---

[53] It is known as *Iwan Dai Jones*.
[54] Welsh: Maer Gan Y Ddraig Ceilliau. The lyrics to this song have been lost to history.

danced incredibly, kicking up her heels and whirling around in rings to the claps of the chorus before she collapses, sweaty and grinning from ear to ear, back into her seat.

She was still grinning as we walked home, arm in arm and more than a little drunk.

'This is a good village full of good people,' she praised as we came near to the castle. 'Some low class people can be quite unfathomable like those three women aboard the train but these people here, your people, they are quite exceptional. I like them all very much.'

This was high praise indeed from a lady who not long before had reckoned that the classes should never mix.

-CHAPTER VIII-

I awoke late the following morning to find that she had vanished.

Belvedere dutifully informed me that, at dawn, she had gone down to the stables along with Sophia but when I retraced their steps there was no sign of either, nor of Evans the horse. Mrs Evans-horse informed me that they had all gone off together in a cart, shouting back the promise that they would all return by noon.

Until they did return I worried. I paced my office, fretting over what it might be that Anna was up to before, at precisely noon, I received a note requesting my presence in the centre of the village. I hurried down the cart track and was relieved to see Anna, safe, outside the oak. I was less relieved by the cartload of expensive looking paintings beside her.

'What the blazes is going on?'

Anna beamed at me and grabbed my arm, dragging me towards the inn.

'I had the idea late last night after I retired so I awoke before dawn and rung for Sophia so that I might be dressed and able to visit the stables. I sent Constance down with a message beforehand so that a horse and cart might be prepared for our arrival. Evans the horse was sniffy at having been woken so early and at having to prepare a cart without notice but when I arrived I explained why this had to be so and he was then more than delighted to play along with my scheme.

'The three of us, that is Evans, Sophia and myself, headed out west and we followed the road up to the Penrhyn house.[55] It was not so far as I might have imagined and we arrived at a frightfully unsociable hour. Not that it mattered since I had checked with Constance to see if she knew that the baron were present. He was not. But the housekeeper was present and awake and she allowed our entry. I must say, Mr Max, that it is not a patch on your own delightful home. It may be more ostentatious and filled with finer furnishings but it is all hollow and without life. It feels less like a home and more of a wild extravagance. If you are required to sleep somewhere it must have heart. Our palace at Ardeluta was far finer but even that had a heart. I did not

---

[55] Its proper name is Penrhyn Castle and is today run by the National Trust.

take to the place.

'The housekeeper asked me why we had come and I explained to her that the Baron Penrhyn had wished for a selection of paintings to be sent to his London residence by that morning's choo-choo. Well she fussed and made quite the palaver I can tell you.

'I have not heard anything of this,' she cried. 'The baron has not informed me!'

'It was an impromptu decision,' explained I before telling her that I was a friend of the baron, Lady Botterly, on my way to Ireland, and that I had promised to pick out several paintings as I passed by for the benefit of the baron. This housekeeper was... What is the word? Gullible? Yes. She was gullible and she fell for my deception completely.

'We three were allowed to wander the castle at our leisure and before we took our choice of the paintings we had a long nose in every room. Evans the horse took a book and a snuff box from the library whilst Sophia and I did the same with any jewellery we came across.'

Anna reached into a pouch at her waist and pulled out what must have been a whole treasure chest of ornaments, necklaces, brooches and assorted gemstones, spreading them across the inn table where we had come to rest whilst she was relating her tale. 'Sophia has much more,' Anna explained. Anna stealing jewellery was one thing, she was not a part of my jurisdiction as far as legal matters were concerned, only her safety was my priority, but I certainly didn't approve of my staff carrying on in that way. I would need to be having strong words with Sophia over this incident, very strong indeed. I would not go so far as to remove her from her post but I would certainly be making sure that she knew how close she had come to such a thing.

Anna continued her tale.

'Once our nose around the castle was done we set to work selecting our paintings. There was one of your old Queen Elizabeth on the wall of a study and well, I decided that such a well disposed lady as she should not be hanging in the residence of a rogue such as Baron Penrhyn. She became the first we seized and whilst we perused other paintings we had the staff take them out to the cart. After Queen Elizabeth we took a landscape. Evans the horse says it is of a mountain called Cadair Idris. And then we found a Van Eyck! Can you believe it? I couldn't. The house keeper protested when I said I wished to take it but I was most insistent on the matter. Mr Evans desired a Turner too, one of Yr Wyddfa, so I promised him he may keep it. Sophia has also expressed a desire for a Rembrandt which we pilfered.'

A REMBRANDT!

I couldn't have my staff claiming other people's Rembrandts on a whim. Lord, I thought to myself, what ever next?

'We claimed around twenty paintings in all. There were some larger ones in the dining room that I wished to have taken but they were too large for the cart. So we only came away with twenty, covered by a large blanket so that people would not see what we had. We came back here as fast as we could, before the staff at the castle could ascertain that we are not who we claimed to be.'

Her story had, by now, attracted a crowd of gawkers, gawkers who had initially entered the pub to see what the cart load of paintings in the road was about. They were all impressed by the gall but I was despairing.

'Miss Anna. You are aware that Penrhyn will move heaven and earth to find those paintings are you not? Well when he finds them, and believe me he *will* find them, he will bring the full might of the law down on whoever has them. He will push for the maximum sentence allowed.'

'You fuss too much Mr Max. He will not find them. Even if he *does* he would not punish a lady of my status.'

'Oh how naïve you are Miss Anna. The baron will not care for your status. He will punish you regardless. And whilst we are on the subject of your status, did you not consider that art theft is an endeavour unbecoming of a well to do lady?'

'Not at all Mr Max. I do not see it as theft. I see it as justice for all the many years of hardship which his family has inflicted upon the land.'

There was an irony here somewhere. Anna was dispensing justice to a corrupt aristocracy and yet here she was hiding from people who, without a doubt, thought they were doing much the same thing. Anna's methods were nowhere near as radical, she had not yet led the quarrymen in a mass uprising, but she was not so far from it as she might have thought.

And what might the consequences of this action be? When Penrhyn found the paintings he would lay the blame at my door, at least to an extent, but then that would be nothing I could not handle. Regarding Anna on the other hand, her

Max & Anna

punishment would be swift and terrible. Penrhyn would have her incarcerated in the darkest cell Caernarfon Gaol had to offer and being in such a place would drive Anna to insanity. She would scream and howl and throw herself against the cold, slimy walls, demanding that a lady of her stature should not be imprisoned, least of all in a festering cess pit like Caernarfon Gaol.[56] Her father would be none too pleased either. Prince Gustaff was not known for his temper but by golly he would fly off the handle if he discovered that I had allowed his daughter to be arrested for theft.

Therefore, certainly, something would have to be done concerning this incident.

I thought of what I might do and left Anna to boast of her exploits to the villagers in the inn and returned to the cart in order to examine the looted paintings. John Douglas was now there, going over them with a fine and appreciative eye. I clapped a hand on his shoulder.

---

[56] In the late nineteenth century Caernarfon Gaol became notorious for its filthy and squalid conditions. It was described in 1895 by local MP, David Lloyd George, (A sort of friend to our family, where he was known as Uncle David) as a 'stinking throwback to the days before the prison reform act.' Max is certainly correct to say that Anna would have been driven insane in such a place.

'John Douglas my friend, what would you suggest we do with these paintings?'

'If I may ask first Mr Morfas, how did they get here? They're from Penrhyn I can see but…'

'It was Miss Anna. This morning she orchestrated a raid on the estate and has only this hour returned with these.'

John Douglas could hardly believe his ears. When I had finished my explanation he circled the cart, examining the paintings and shaking his head.

'This could be bad Mr Morfas. If the baron catches us with these he'll have the whole village thrown into Caernarfon Gaol, Miss Anna the pint included. Now usually I would recommend returning these, theft is against God's law after all, but this is the Baron Penrhyn and a part of me wants to see him bleed. If any man deserved to have his paintings stolen it would be he. So I won't recommend you give them back… Still, we cannot be caught with these. We should remove the canvases from the frames and then destroy the frames. We'll hide the canvasses in the castle basement. No policeman could find them there. Now… Does anyone up at Penrhyn know that it was Miss Anna who took the paintings?'

'Unfortunately yes. She somehow managed to persuade the housekeeper that she was Lady Botterly, a friend of the baron.'

'This housekeeper could point the finger at Miss Anna then. We must deal with her. We must ensure her silence.'

I was in complete agreement with what he said and whilst Anna, John Douglas and some of the villagers set to work removing and breaking up the frames I had the housekeeper of Penrhyn sent for.

It was an hour before she arrived and although by now the paintings themselves had been hidden the remains of the frames were still in plain sight, lying in easily combustible pieces by the door of the inn. As she approached she stared at them with curiosity and then, as she got to them, picked one up. Immediately recognising it she let out a shriek of calumny and began to run for her cart. John Douglas stepped from a cottage door and blocked her path, then wheeling her back in the direction of the inn.

'Those frames... They belong to the baron! What have you done? You stole them... Oh lord have mercy on you all when the baron finds out.'

Entering the inn she saw Anna and myself at a table and

recognized Anna for the thief. She pointed her finger in an accusatory fashion.

'You... You're the one who came and took the paintings. You stole them! Oh lord have mercy on your soul when the baron finds out.' I reached forwards and gently seated her in a chair. She was so flustered that she was only too grateful for my help.

'The baron is not going to find out... I am sorry, I do not know your name. Mrs?'

'Hillier. Mrs Hillier.[57] And the baron *will* find out sir. I sent him a telegram saying that his paintings had been sent, just this morning after this lady departed.'

'And what, Mrs Hillier, do you imagine he will do when he learns of the stolen paintings?'

'He'll bring the whole law down on this godless, sinful village you mark my words.'

'And what, Mrs Hillier, shall happen to yourself?' Mrs Hillier looked into my eyes for a moment and then screeched.

'Oh lord have mercy on my soul... He shall remove me from my post for allowing his paintings to be stolen. Oh lord

---

[57] Hatshepsut Hillier- Born in Chester, 1820.

have mercy on my soul! What ever shall I do?'

'Calm yourself Mrs Hillier. Things shall not be so terrible as you believe. At least they shall not if you accept the generous offer which I am about to make you.' She stopped floundering and became inquisitive.

On the table before me I had a pile of papers and I slid the topmost over to Mrs Hillier, which she read with interest. I shall describe to you, in short, the details it contained. In exchange for Mrs Hillier never revealing to another living soul that it was Miss Anna who stole the paintings from Penrhyn I would offer her a job that paid her one and a half times the rate of her present salary.[58] The infirmary at Bangor was in sore need of staff at that time and I believed Mrs Hillier would make an excellent matron. She would only require references and a trial period of employment but these were trivial affairs. I could provide the references and her current role as housekeeper would have already provided ample training for a matron's position. The roles are not so different after all. The only difference between

---

[58] Records indicate that she was earning thirteen shillings per week whilst working for the Baron Penrhyn. This was around the same average wage as a farm hand.

them is that one requires more of a bedside manner than the other, and not necessarily a good one.

Mrs Hillier examined the paper before her and then gave an appreciable nod.

'This seems fair. But what of care of employment?'

'You shall be better cared for than in your current position Mrs Hillier, I assure you.'

'And where would I live?'

'That we shall have to arrange. However, I am friends with the Earl of Beddgelert and he owns several houses in Bangor and lets them at reasonable rates. They are good houses too, so I am told.' Mrs Hillier puffed herself up and presented a snobbish air.

'I want *twice* my current pay and not a penny less.' I smiled. For her silence it was worth every penny.

On the coldest night of that year those frames heated the village and in a land where the nearest available wood is a five mile walk or from a costly travelling merchant this was a godsend and everyone was grateful. As for the paintings themselves… Well I shall come to them in due course.

-CHAPTER IX-

Later that afternoon Anna and I drove out to Conwy on the northern coast. Upon seeing the castle she made one of her customary remarks.

'It must surely have been impressive once upon a time. I will admit it is a nicer castle than the house of the Baron Penrhyn but not nearly so nice as Cythry.'

'You know, the architect, Master James of St George... It is reckoned that he took some of his inspiration for this place from Cythry.'

'Is that so?' She gave a nod and as we were touring the castle she asked me to point to the parts that were inspired by Cythry.

Sadly, I could not. As much as I tried to look for something that resembled my home there was absolutely nothing. I had been brought up on this idea, that Conwy castle was inspired by Cythry, but I had never before assumed that it might be false. Now that I looked and saw the truth, that the old claim *was* false, that it was little more than a tall tale, I was most aggrieved. Anna tried to soothe my despair with some kind words.

'Do not be gloomy Mr Max. He could never have achieved the same grandeur as Cythry anyhow. Even if he had tried he would have been a disastrous failure.' Those words were of little comfort for the loss of an idea which I had long held and treasured.

After touring the castle we sat in a tea room for a short while. The rain had started to fall for the first time since Anna had arrived. There are some who will tell you that it *always* rains in Wales but this is simply not true. It is just that when it does rain it rains hard and often without warning. There is also a peculiar natural phenomena known as 'Welsh rain' which to my knowledge only happens in this part of the world. The sun can be shining in the heavens and the sky could be as blue and cloudless as the Mediterranean yet for a reason that baffles even the greatest scientific minds on the planet it can *still* and often *does* begin to rain.[59]

This particular shower began as Welsh rain as we were

---

[59] This phenomena is also called 'Serein' and despite Max's claim it is not unique to Wales. It happened to me in Prague last summer, for example. It also happens to James whenever he wants to put the laundry out.

leaving the castle and Anna stopped to look up into the near cloudless sky.

'How is it raining?' she asked, confounded. 'Where are the clouds? Should there not be clouds for it to begin raining?'

'In any other part of the world certainly. But this is Wales. The usual laws of physics do not apply here.' I was teasing but she thought me serious and laughed.

'What utter tummy rot Mr Max. The laws of physics apply everywhere. They are constant... Unless you are calling my girlhood tutor a liar?' I continued to tease.

'No. Not at all. The laws of physics *are* constant. I was merely stating that Wales appears to be an exception to the rule. Such as with the rain for instance.'

By the time we had reached the tea room the Welsh rain had transformed to regular rain, coming down in great waterfalls from a sky that was thick with black clouds. Anna was much happier about this and her delight at that moment was accusing me of falsehoods concerning the laws of physics.

'It cannot rain whilst there are no clouds in the sky. Whatever we felt earlier must have blown in on the wind from wherever this present storm happened to be at the time.' I didn't wish to contradict her but had been *no wind* at the time. It had been an almost universally perfect summer's day. That rain had not blown in on the wind, it was thoroughly Welsh in its origins. Anna would not accept, however, that this was an actual phenomena. 'Mr Max. There must be some explanation for what occurred. I cannot believe it.'

We continued to argue over the existence of Welsh rain, in between china cups of tea and scones, before the clouds lifted and we could once more set foot out of doors without being soaked to the bone.

We left Conwy and drove the length of the river, where we stopped briefly in the town of Llanrwst so that I could show Anna the empty sarcophagus of Llewelyn ap Iorwerth. She joked that the reason it was empty was that Llewelyn was another defier of the physical laws and that he had somehow removed himself from the coffin after death, wanting a better place to be buried. We strolled the town after this visit, for it is a pleasant place, before returning to the cart.

At Betws Y Coed, yet further down the river and where we would turn west for home, we admired the work of some artists painting by the road side, but not for long. I'd had quite enough of paintings for one day and as the shadows were starting to lengthen it was high time we were returning to Cythry. Anna was highly aggrieved that we did not stay in Betws for very long and she made no end of noise about it as we drove away.

'Really Mr Max, your behaviour borders on the frightful. That village, what did you call it? Well whatever, it does not matter, but it looked to be a beautiful place. Why could we not stay there for a short while? Why could we not look around?'

'Miss Anna,' I snapped. 'It grows late and you have had a long day. It is time we were both retiring for the evening and not gallivanting around places like Betws.' She folded her arms in protest.

'Then I shall have Mr Evans the horse take me back there when we arrive at Cythry. I shall walk the streets without you.'

'And what do you intend to see?' By the time you have returned from Cythry it shall be pitch dark and you shall not be able to see a bloody thing. Add to this, a lady should not wander alone at night. People will get the wrong impression.'

'I shall not be wandering alone. I shall have Evans the horse to escort me.'

She was wrong on that front. Evans the horse would not escort her.

'It is getting far too late to be driving out to Betws Miss Anna. This yon horse you've had pulling this cart is tired and I've already put the others to bed.' Anna stamped her feet in the most childlike way and then stormed off to the castle.

When we entered through the doors she made a declaration.

'We shall go first thing in the morning, after breakfast. Does that suit your tastes Mr Max?'

'Yes Miss Anna. That is perfectly acceptable.'

Therefore, following breakfast the next morn, we drove back out to Betws and Anna was quite adamant that we remain for as long as was possible, a whole day in her opinion. At the time I could think of nothing more dull than spending an entire day in Betws. It is certainly nice to look at and wander through for an hour or so but not for an entire day. Yet with Anna it became immensely enjoyable and not dull in the slightest.

Max & Anna

First we seated ourselves by the river, near to the bridge, and watched a group of children playing at 'Trolls' beneath. They would hide underneath and then jump out and roar when someone passed by, much to their own amusement and also to that of their unsuspecting Billy goats. Anna also found it amusing, though I merely found it charming. What it must be to be so young and without responsibility, to be so full of life. I cannot recall any longer but those children knew it all too well.

The children went away after a period leaving Anna and myself to recline by the river and to watch it flow by and to listen to the sounds of the water cascading over rocks and boulders. But soon, as those children before us, we too left the river and we wandered the village at our leisure. We spoke to several others on our travels. Anna insisted on greeting them with a 'bore da,' even when they were not Welsh. I'll admit, it struck up more than a few conversation pieces with people asking if she lived in these parts. The story changed every time but that was no great matter. So long as there was a story and she was not revealing that she was a Romanian princess all was well.

We took a guided stroll into the forest of Gwydir where we

were told all sorts of fanciful tales about the elves and the pixies and the creatures who dwelt there. I had heard them all many times before and knew them by heart but to Anna they were new and thrilling and she loved every instance that she was informed of a fairy ring or an elf pool or a supposedly enchanted tree. We were taken as far as Llyn Y Sarnau before turning back.

We walked Betws once more, lord knows why but I can at least say it was pleasant, before we found ourselves in the studio of a photographer. It was Anna's request. She expressed a desire to have her photograph taken with me so that she might have a keepsake of her time in Wales. As we had little clue as to how long she would be staying with me I agreed, ordering two copies of the photograph so that I too would have a keepsake, a reminder of the stubborn, insistent, snobbish but ultimately enchanting princess whom I had been assigned to protect.

-CHAPTER X-

Arriving back at Cythry there awaited us a telegram from the Earl of Beddgelert. He had acquired a box at the opera house in Bangor for that evening. It was to be the opening night of a new Welsh language opera.[60] I had not heard of such a thing taking place but the idea sounded intriguing.

The only cloud on the horizon preventing attendance were those dreadful revolutionaries. Strolling around and admiring places such as Betws was one thing but it was a thing so innocuous and unpredictable that we could get away with it. Unless they were constantly observing us or there was a spy in my household, neither of which I believed to be true, they would not know for certain where they might strike at us unless by an unfortunate coincidence. The opera on the other hand, and opening night no less, might well be the sort of place they would expect her to be and it was somewhere they could easily lie in wait in order to

---

[60] Despite its purported magnificence, the opera (Constantine) never took off outside of Wales and never gained much in the way of popularity. The last known performance was in Cardiff in 1912 and today only three copies of the manuscript survive, all kept in the National Library of Wales.

spring a trap.

Then again, I had not seen any sign that the revolutionaries were present in the area. They were keeping well hidden if they were there. Over the previous few days I had kept my eye open at all times for anyone suspicious and I had seen no one. There had been no reports from either my staff or the villagers of strangers roaming the land and had Gyddyn or his fellow Frodorion noted any suspicious characters lurking about the hills they would have been certain to inform me.

This brought me to the inevitable conclusion that, for the moment, we were safe and that it would be a perfectly acceptable thing to take Anna to the opera. She was overjoyed.

Bangor's opera house was in the portion of the city known as 'Upper Bangor.' The main thoroughfare through the district is called Ffordd Caergybi and it was against this road, which is a fashionable road I should add, that you could find the opera house. It was one of a pair of buildings that stood on either side of the entrance to a side road. The other was the church of Penrallt and today *that* building still stands. Alas, in the year eighteen eighty four the opera house was destroyed by fire and as much as I have attempted to persuade the city council of the need for a replacement none has been forthcoming.[61] When it stood the opera house was the twin to the church and was near identical. The only difference was a façade of neoclassical columns which supported a larger portico than that of the church. In all other respects it was the same. It may have been architecturally insignificant in comparison to its operatic peers but it was, regardless, a wonder.

Beddgelert and his lady wife were awaiting us under the portico as we arrived. She was a divine, angelic beauty[62] and he was a charming, pot bellied beast of a man. To look at them you would not think them suited but that they were and never were a couple more so.

Beddgelert saw us disembarking our carriage, driven by Belvedere, and came down the steps to greet us.

'Max my dear chap how are you?' He shook me vigorously by the hand. 'And this must be... GOOD GOD! PRINCESS

---

[61] It was a performance of the very same opera opening that night which caused the fire that destroyed the building. Today, in its place, stands a café and a bar.

[62] Lady Beddgelert at this time was Plurabelle Cadbury-Cavendish, second daughter of a Marquess of Kidderminster.

ANNA OF ARDELUTA!'

'Beddgelert, please! Keep your voice down,' I urged, hoping that nobody else had heard his ejaculation. He understood the need and gave a signal of assent to show that he would keep his voice down.

'Max my dear chap… According to the papers this lady is being hunted by ruthless men. They want her head and they have made no secret of it.'

'I am quite aware of them, though I am certain that they *do not* know she is here right now. They are in fact the reason she is here. She is under my protection and we would appreciate that nobody learns of her true identity on the slight chance that those ruthless men come searching for her.' He bowed to us.

'Then you have my discretion. Miss Anna, it is a pleasure to meet you.'

'Thank you. Tell me Mr Beddgelert… How was it that you were able to recognize me?'

'I am a follower of the continental newspapers Miss Anna. The revolution in Ardeluta has not been reported on here in Britain but in parts of Europe it is major news. I recalled your face from a picture in an Italian newspaper.'

'I see. Well so long as nobody else in these parts has read the continental newspapers then all should be satisfactory.'

'I know of nobody else who does Miss Anna. As you say, all should be satisfactory. Now perhaps you would like to be introduced to Lady Beddgelert?'

'Yes please. That would be most charming.'

It was an instant attraction between the two women. Lady Beddgelert and Anna were all smiles as soon as they set eyes upon each other, followed by a kiss upon the cheek and a bore da. They began admiring the clothing of the other and Anna began to tell of our exploits in the wardrobe at Cythry, lamenting that I kept some truly rotten attire in there. Beddgelert and I, meanwhile, walked to the far side of the portico so that we might have our own discussion.

'Precisely what is this opera which is opening tonight?' I asked. 'I have heard nothing of any new Welsh language opera.'

'Nor had I until this morning. Apparently they only booked the house yesterday. They came up from Cardiff because the opera house down there was flooded out and there is no other in the principality.'

'Well… Cardiff's loss is our gain.'

'Indeed. I think you will like this opera Max. It's about Constantine.'

'The emperor or the king?'

'The king. It should make for quite an interesting opera in my opinion.'

'Yes. Welsh language too! Golly!'

'Only the third ever written would you believe? Makes one feel quite proud to be in attendance.'

'Well god bless whoever wrote it!'

Constantine, since I were a child, has been a hero of mine. He was a warrior of skill and virtue brought low by a quest for vengeance. He was one of the knights of the round table and one of the seven survivors of Camlann. Legend holds that after Arthur's death Constantine, who was his successor, orchestrated a quest to hunt down any last remaining supporters of Mordred. He became so blinded by this quest that he neglected his duties as king and all of Arthur's hard won prosperity fell to rack and ruin. Constantine fell to vices and sin, even casting his queen to a nunnery in favour of a younger and more supple woman. After some years he came upon the sons of Mordred inside of a church and he sundered them a terrible and violent death. According to that celebrated historian, Geoffrey of Monmouth, it was several years more before he was wrought down by divine retribution, usurped by his nephew Aurelius Conanus. I do not like this version of the tale myself and it is not in the North Walian tradition. That North Walian tradition dictates that it was in the church of Llantyswlio where he, Constantine, came upon the sons of Mordred and as he made the final blow he was struck by a heavenly bolt of lightning as retribution. I prefer the local version as it is more dramatic.

Entering the opera house for the opening of the performance, the ladies before us and chattering like old friends, Beddgelert came in close to me.

'Did you hear about what happened at Penrhyn yesterday morning?'

'No. Is it exciting? Do tell!' I placed my best, most intrigued look upon my face.

'It seems that yesterday morning a lady with a foreign accent turned up claiming that the baron wanted some paintings sent down to London. He'd done no such thing of course and this lady got clean away with twenty of his best paintings.'

'Gosh. How terrible. Do we know how the baron has taken the news?'

'That I do not know my friend. But I would assume not well. From what I hear half of his staff have handed in their notice so as to avoid his wrath.'

'Really? And it was a lady with a foreign accent you say?' We both looked in Anna's direction.

'I highly doubt that someone of Miss Anna's calibre would resort to stealing paintings... But on the chance, where was she yesterday morning?'

'With myself. We breakfasted down by the lake and then she accompanied me on my rounds.'

'Then I think that we can safely assume she is not the culprit in this instance.'

We took our seats in one of the boxes. Bangor's opera house only had four, two on each side of the stage, and ours was to the rear on the right hand side. I was glad it was to the rear as the boxes at the front were too close to the stage and you had to crane your neck over the edge just to get a decent view. All you could see otherwise was the audience and it is not so fun to watch *them* as it is to watch the opera. The seats were in better condition here too. They were not so worn nor so uncomfortable as the ones in the boxes nearer to the stage.

Anna and I seated ourselves next to each other and we both felt the other tingle as a messianic chorus exploded from the stage and the curtains opened to reveal a scene of apocalyptic majesty. Armour clad warriors pounced onto the stage from either side and their swords clashed as the strains of the messianic chorus grew louder and more intense before it ceased abruptly. The warriors parted as a fog descended across the stage and through them stepped two gigantic men who towered over the other performers, Arthur and Mordred. The two pointed their swords at each other, Arthur's was Excalibur of course, and they traded barbed insults before the warriors clashed once more and the messianic chorus started anew. This time it was joined by the might of Arthur and Mordred coming to blows, trading operatic slurs between each clash of their sword.

The warriors died one by one and eventually only Arthur and Mordred were left on the stage. By this point the slurs had ceased and the chorus had been replaced by a terrifying, heart stopping cacophony from the loudest instruments of the orchestra, the drums and the oboes and the cymbals.

Their combat was a frightening ballet and the performers must have their due for the high skill which they displayed. Sweat was pouring from their brows and the look of anger and concentration upon their faces was certainly genuine. One could have been forgiven for thinking that they were the real Arthur and Mordred.

It ended as only it could, with the loud thundering of the drums as Mordred stabbed Arthur through the chest and then the aforementioned Arthur did likewise, only with the addition of a tenorial spiel. Mordred was brought low and the music sank with him. He and Arthur gave one another an aria of forgiveness before Mordred finally dropped down dead and Arthur collapsed into the arms of his surviving warriors, who came onto the stage at precisely the right moment. With one last and lengthy aria Arthur arranged his affairs, Bedevere returning Excalibur to the lady of the lake and the like, and then he looked on of the soldiers above him and stroked his cheek.

'Constantine my son,' he sang (I am again translating from the Welsh) 'I give you my kingdom. Look after it and rule it wisely.' Knowing the story a surge of dread washed over me. Then Arthur died.

As the lights on the stage dimmed the house blew up into thunderous applause. Anna and myself were amongst the loudest. That had only been the first scene and it had been spectacular, a real triumph. It raised the bar for the remainder of the performance to such a height that I did not think that it could live up to my expectations. But how wrong I was. The opera only grew better and more powerful as the now King Constantine began his quest for vengeance and his descent into sin and madness. I could not take my eyes of the stage until the interval.

The first act ended with the casting out of the queen and I could feel her pain to such a degree that I nearly began to weep alongside her. Our two ladies were weeping and as the lights rose for the interval and the house was again filled with rapturous applause they wiped their eyes with silk handkerchiefs and said 'how silly we are being. It is *only* an opera but here we are blubbering like school children.' There was no shame in it as they were not the only ones. Outside in the entrance hall and on the portico we saw other ladies who were red around the eyes and wiping themselves with silk handkerchiefs.

The opera was all anybody could talk about and I heard

not a word said against it. Anna was seconds short of bouncing around, declaring that although she had not understood a single word it was one of the most magnificent operas which she had ever seen. She even said that it was stupendous enough to put Wagner to shame, to make him appear insignificant. The rest of us were in profound agreement.

It was a notion reinforced by the second act and the spectacle only intensified as Constantine's quest for vengeance reached its apex. The performer portraying him had a real streak of madness within himself and he brought this right to the fore, making my childhood hero seem more animal than man.

The music ascended and continued to ascend to such a height that the building trembled. I felt Anna take hold of my hand in fear, and I took hold of hers, and we did not let go again until the curtain had descended and the opera was done.

During the final scene, which was a riot of blood and gore, we were squeezing each other so tightly that I thought our hands might burst. It was the most terrifying thing that I had ever seen. Constantine charged onto the stage where the sons of Mordred were looting the church and with his sword held aloft he destroyed them several times over. They being well and truly dead he dropped his sword and began to sing a triumphal song of victory, one that demonstrated his insanity and just how far he had fallen since Arthur proclaimed him king during the first scene. Then the messianic chorus from that opening scene flared up once more as Constantine picked up a chalice that was in the process of being looted by the sons of Mordred. He filled it with altar wine and declared that by God's will he had slain the last of Mordred's supporters. As he placed the chalice to his lips and drank the stage lit up and the whole opera house shook as the king was struck by lightning and all that remained of where he had been standing was smoke, the chalice and the fallen sons of Mordred.[63] There was no music, only silence, and the curtain descended.

The house was struck dumb by the awe of it all and then everybody clapped as though their lives depended on it.

---

[63] The idea of 'the chalice' appears to have been created specifically for the opera as it appears in no source or oral tradition prior to the date of the opening night. It is, however, frequently mentioned in Edwardian literature concerning the subject and around 1910 a replica chalice was created.

That was truly the best opera anybody there had ever seen. It was so good that none of us, that is nobody in the entire house, knew what to say even as we decamped to our various homes and carriages awaiting outside. We were all so enraptured and so mesmerized by the spectacle which we had witnessed. The only words I heard spoken were by myself and Beddgelert as myself and Anna climbed into our carriage.

'You and Miss Anna will come dine at Beddgelert Hall tomorrow evening won't you Max?'

'Yes. That would be splendid.'

By the time I entered the carriage proper Anna was fast asleep, no doubt dreaming of Constantine and his magnificent opera. I too would dream of it that night and for many more afterwards.

-CHAPTER XI-

Somewhere on the mountain of Tryfan there is rumoured to be a cave where King Arthur and his knights sleep.[64] Anna, inspired by our night at the opera, had scoured the library for books on Constantine and she came across this small piece of trivia in the process. It intrigued her and she begged me to help her search for the cave. I had planned to show her Llanberis and perhaps row on one of the lakes there but a walk around the lower slopes of Tryfan, searching for this cave, was a more inviting prospect.

We took with us a lunch of sandwiches, ginger beer, cold meats and cheese, all placed into a knapsack, and we set out at ten on the morning after. John Douglas accompanied us out of the village as he had business in Bethesda. We parted company at the Ogwen road, he walking along it and we crossing over to the Glyderau opposite.

It is a very different feeling, wandering the Glyderau to wandering the Carneddau. It is more claustrophobic, in so

---

[64] Some sources reckon it is instead Merlin or Arthur and Bedevere or even just Bedevere alone.

far as a mountain range can *be* claustrophobic, and it makes one feel smaller and more insignificant over there. On that particular morning their peaks were covered by low clouds and the feeling of claustrophobic insignificance loomed large over us.

We entered the range by a stile in a dry stone wall and after crossing a brook by way of a neatly placed stone to act as a bridge we walked for a good twenty minutes across gently rising grassland and the lower slopes before we came to Tryfan, or more specifically the cwm that lay before it.[65] After paying homage to this great beast by sketching it in pads we had brought for the occasion, Anna's sketch was superior to mine but neither were worthy of hanging in a gallery, we headed along the stream there and strained our eyes upwards, trying to locate the cave.

'It would be silly of them to bury people in a high cave. Who would want to carry a corpse all the way up a mountain?' Anna espoused after five or ten minutes of this. 'The cave must be low. We must search low if we wish to find it.'

'There was a young man who reckoned to have found it

---

[65] Known as Cwm Tryfan.

once upon a time,' I informed. 'This was well back in history you understand… When he found it he marked the spot and left a trail back to the place but when he returned the next day his trail was gone and he never found the cave again.'

'It was those Frodorion no doubt. They ruined his trail out of spite.'

'The Frodorion are not a spiteful people Miss Anna. Besides, some sources even reckon the young man was a Frodorion.'

'Well *somebody* must have moved the trail. If not the Frodorion then perhaps Merlin. Perhaps he did it to guard Arthur's tomb.' It was a good suggestion and I liked it, though the thought of Merlin roaming the Glyderau and guarding Arthur's tomb after all these years was a silly and absurd notion when you really considered it.

Around midday we came to the end of the cwm and came to the highest point of our trek, the southern flank of Tryfan where the mountain joins with Glyder Fach behind. As yet we had seen no trace of the cave. It was here that we stopped to eat our picnic and to make more sketches. It was the same story as earlier in the case of the latter. Anna's sketch was superior to mine though neither was of a high enough standard to be hung on the walls of a gallery.

It was also at this stage that I came over all queer. I came to the idea that I was enjoying Anna's company to such a degree that I did not want our trek to end. I did not wish to return to Cythry or the society of others and I certainly did not wish to dine with Beddgelert that evening, not that I had anything against him mind. I wanted only to be alone with Anna, there in those mountains, and I wanted to impress her with stories like that of the young man who had discovered the cave only never to find his way back again. I wanted to hear her spiky reposts to those stories and I wished to debate with her concerning them, coming to absurd conclusions such as that Merlin was roaming the hills, still guarding Arthur's tomb.

At her worst she was a snobbish prig, a lady who sneered at the people beneath her and who had some peculiar ideas about the social classes. At the same time I had witnessed her behave in a manner that was completely contradictory to these ideas. I had seen her freely mixing with the villagers of Cythry and I had seen her dancing with them and launching a bold raid against their most hated foe. She was bossy and she demanded to have things her own way but I was growing fond of that aspect of her nature. It set her apart from other women whom I had known, many of whom were weak and demure and with little hold over their own independence. They would all give it up as easily as plum pie, though not Anna. If someone made a serious blow against *her* independence then she would fight them for it, most likely using her teeth.

I had observed her reactions when the situation called for her to be unobtrusive, such as on the train, and when she had taken against the idea in question. That had been bad enough for me and I would not have liked to be on the receiving end if ever I had done anything to *seriously* impede her independence.

At her best she was a dear, sweet thing. I adored those moments when she was at her happiest and most gleeful, that morning in the mountains or during the previous night at the opera. She was childlike in her joy and it was an infectious thing. When she was happy I too was happy and I would have done almost anything to ensure her happiness so long as it did not bring her near to any harm.

We descended back to the Ogwen road, a steep descent from the conjunction of the mountains which took us past

Llyn Bochlwyd. Here I could not help but observe Anna's every move and the way in which she held herself. Her posture was always high and straight backed, she never once slouched, and her aura was one of uptight morality. She did not look the sort of lady who went about stealing paintings from the landed gentry. Every footstep she made was carefully considered and she moved with grace and poise. Even when she was marching ahead or as I was helping her across a boggy or steep piece of ground she retained this elegance. She was a lady of class and that would be the case whatever her situation, whatever clothes she happened to wear. Had she been a working class girl, and despite what I state above she was perfectly capable of passing as one, then she would have been one of those who become the cornerstone of their community, one of those who are loved and admired by all.

Near to the road I came across a Snowdon Lilly, a rare flower, and I plucked it from the ground and gave it to Anna.[66] She adored it and called it one of the prettiest flowers existing upon the earth. With my help she placed it

---

[66] Please do not do this yourself as the Snowdon Lilly is a rare and protected species.

inside a button hole near to the top of her dress. Then she wanted find one for myself so that we would match but as much as she scouted around in the nearby area she could not find another. They were as elusive as that cave upon the mountain.

As we walked back along the Ogwen road we continued to search for that cave but saw no trace of it. There came a point where we thought we might have discovered it, hanging low on the north ridge about one hundred metres up, but it was no more than an illusion.

'Ooh,' Anna clapped and pointed. 'Is that it Mr Max?' I followed her finger and noticed a long, interesting cleft in the rock. I scrambled up from the roadside and Anna followed suit. We were both most excited and thrilled at the prospect of going down in history as the people who discovered Arthur's tomb. It was a steady climb and we had to scramble up the last part but our arrival only resulted in a heavy disappointment. It was nothing more than a deep crag with the rear obscured by shadow.

Our disappointment was short lived. On the way back down to the road once more I made the suggestion that it had been Merlin's doing. The cave *had* been there but he had sealed it off to prevent us from entering. It would open again, no doubt, when our backs were turned. We both laughed and came to the conclusion that Merlin must be watching us and so we tried to see if we could spy him. He hid from us, of course, but it was jolly fun searching and a marvellous end to the walk.

Before I move on I must add this. When we finally reached Cythry I asked Anna if when she departed my company after the revolutionaries had dissipated she would ever return to visit.

'Do you mean visit yourself or the land? The truth is, Mr Max, that I do not know. The future is unknowable and so until I return who is to say that I will? What I do know is that I shall never forget you, Mr Max. You have sometimes been a brute but you have also brought me much joy and happiness. I *hope* that one day I shall come back.'

Her words were enough to satisfy me. To know that there was always the chance I would see her again was enough.

-CHAPTER XII-

Dinner parties are such dull affairs. Not to attend- If that were the case then they would never happen at all- but in hindsight, to write of and remember. What of interest *is there* for one to write of? The journey to the place of dining perhaps?

Certainly not in the case of mine and Anna's journey to Beddgelert hall which took an hour and was mostly uneventful. The only thing of interest to say on the matter of the journey is that we passed by Yr Wyddfa but the events of the day were clouding my mind like a flock of butterflies and in my mental wanderings I forgot to point it out to Anna. I only came to the realization of my forgetfulness as I brought our cart to the gates of Beddgelert hall, a not quite imposing mansion of the late Tudor period, set in an L shaped pattern over two floors.[67] I slapped my forehead in the disbelief that I had forgotten to show my companion such an important part of my hand.

---

[67] Beddgelert Hall was originally built in 1596 by Gwydion ap Goronwy, first Earl of Beddgelert. It was later abandoned and eventually demolished in 1958.

'Oh Miss Anna,' I confessed, 'I have done a most dreadful thing. I am afraid I forgot to point Yr Wyddfa to you on the way down here when I really should have done so.'

'Was it the large mountain on the right? If so it was a most horrible thing. It did not look a wholesome or picturesque mountain.'

'Which mountain would this be?' Beddgelert had come out from the hall to greet us and had overheard Anna's remarks.

'Yr Wyddfa. Mr Max was saying how he forgot to point it out but I caught sight of it anyway.'

'Ah. Your opinions may be because you saw it from the road and at close quarters. It is better seen from a distance. Here, let me show you.'

He took her by the arm and guided us both into the courtyard of the hall from where we would have a direct view of the mountain, a view which I always forget is there. I forget because the hall itself faces towards Cnict, a mountain with a finer profile than Yr Wyddfa, and in order to see Yr Wyddfa one must stand in a particular place. Beddgelert hall is surrounded by trees you see and there is but one spot on the northern side where the gap between them is large enough to see the mountain. Despite only being across the far side of Beddgelert village it looks to be more distant than it actually is. This, I believe, is to do with the height of the mountain causing an optical illusion, making it appear further away than reality dictates. Anna was still not in the least bit impressed by it.

'It is an ungodly lump,' she huffed before making her own way into the hall.

We had a splendid evening, though as I mentioned in my opening paragraph there was very little of interest to write of. It began in the usual way that dinner parties do, with drinks in the drawing room where we talked with Beddgelert, his lady wife and the others who were to dine with us that evening. They were Monsignor Hywell, a catholic priest and the only one I knew of to reside between Chester and Dublin; Roderick ap Eryri, a well to do farmer but who was too much of a pompous bore for my liking; his own lady wife who was Scottish and much like her husband; and a spinster by the name of Millway, who was a daughter of the vicar of Nantmor. These people are not important so I will not describe them in any more detail, nor shall I enter into any aspects of our conversation for it was of the banal kind that one usually has before dining. I should be quite amazed if I could still recall any of it.

I cannot even, to tell you fairly, recall what was eaten when we entered the dining room. I know that lamb was involved and I know the meal included gravy but only for what Anna did with it. It was not the good kind of gravy, the kind the name of gravy suggests it should be, not the thick and gloopy kind that is a deep and blocky colour. A mustardy hue is my preferred choice but I will accept a chocolate brown if it is of the right consistency. This gravy was a light brown and it was so thin that as to be water.

Anna picked up the gravy boat without so much as a second thought and poured it onto her plate in the same manner that the Moroccans pour tea, from a height. Needless to say, its watery consistency meant that it splattered and splashed all over the plate and table but managed to somehow avoid any of the guests. Anna squealed and righted the jug before any more mess could be caused and she set the boat back on the table as though it had offended her. The other dinner guests stared at her, wondering what she had been doing, but she ignored them and carried on as though she had behaved in a regular manner.

For her it was normal of course. Ardelutian custom has it that gravy is thick (and I agree) and poured out slowly, from a height, dripping onto the plate like tar. Anna had not expected the gravy to be so thin.

She pouted at the result and sulked before her plate.

'Oh dear. Now my lamb is swimming. Lady Beddgelert, I hope you do not take offence but I find that your gravy is far too watery for my liking.' She looked around the table for a moment and caught sight of an empty wine glass by Mrs Roderick. Snatching it up she proceeded to pour all the watery gravy from her plate into that glass before handing it to a member of staff. 'Here, take this away. And bring another glass to replace the once I have just used.' Her order was carried out and nobody again mentioned the incident.

After dinner the gentlemen and the ladies separated as is customary, we gentlemen remaining in the dining room for port whilst the ladies retired to the drawing room. I found the port to be the dullest part of the evening and I could not wait to be done so that I might escape the pomposity and boredom of Roderick ap Eryri. The man was frightful and all others in the room thought so too. Why Beddgelert invited him I shall never understand.

After we rejoined the ladies Anna and I did not linger long. The drive back to Cythry was a lengthy one and the mountain roads could be deadly at night. The road between Beddgelert and Pen y Gwryd where it reaches the pass of Llanberis and the border with Morfasson country is notorious for bandits and I did not wish to encounter them, for Anna's sake. We stayed long enough to be polite but that was all.

We bid adieu to the Beddgelerts and our fellow guests then proceeded to return to Cythry.

We returned to our worst nightmare.

-CHAPTER XIII-

Evans the horse was waiting by the stables as we arrived and his look was one of absolute fright.

'Mr Morfas sir, you're wanted up at the castle right away. We've just sent a telegram to Beddgelert Hall asking for your return but thank God you were already on the way back. It's Codswallop sir. He just got back from London but he got off the train at Aber and he ran here over the mountains.'

'Why on earth did he do a silly thing like that?'

'I don't know Mr Morfas sir but he was in quite the state when he got to the castle. He said he needs to talk to you right away.'

I snapped the reins of the horse who was pulling our cart and raced us up to the castle in record speed. We were going so fast that that I almost brought us crashing down over the side of the cart track. Our horse, thank goodness, knew where he was going and he kept us safe and on the right path, stopping at precisely the right point before the doors of Cythry.

'Where is he?' I demanded of Belvedere who came rushing

out of the door as I helped Anna down from the cart.

'He is in the drawing room sir. John Douglas and Gyddyn y Dulyn are with him.' I ejaculated in surprise.

'Gyddyn? Why on earth would he be here?'

'I do not know sir. He arrived not long after Mr Codswallop.'

Christ, I thought to myself. Two visits from him inside of a week! If he had come again then things must be serious indeed.

'Get this cart down to the stables and hurry back here,' I ordered.

Belvedere bowed to my order and as the horse and cart clattered away, back down the track, I ran inside with Anna at close quarters. She squealed when we collided with Gyddyn at the foot of the staircase.

'It is quite alright Miss Anna. This is Gyddyn. He is harmless, I assure you.' She took a cautious step backwards, away from him. He held his hands up to show he was not armed and then bowed his head. Then he spoke in English, a rare thing for a Frodorion.

'I am not a man of violence Miss Anna. I only act against those who have offended myself or my people or our livelihoods and you have done none of those things. I shall do you no harm.'

His words did little to reassure her. She took another step away from him.

'Why have you come?'

'I saw your man, Faban-Morfa. I saw him run across the high plain in a desperate panic. I called out but he would not stop. I came because his state brought dread to my heart. I fear. I fear because the portents of death have grown stronger.' Anna backed away into a corner.

'What portents of death?'

Anna trembled.

'Dreams of blood, Miss Anna, the blood of my people and those of Faban-Morfa. Not only the dreams, but *he* has been heard also. The reaper of *Death* stalks the mountains and he sings his lament in full.'

'His lament?'

'At the beginning of the world Death was but a mortal man and he fell in love with a beautiful woman. She departed from him due to the machinations of wicked men, never to return to his arms. In her absence he became hollow and empty. Years later he was to learn of her premature death and the man who would become Death mourned her passing to such a degree that he journeyed to the underworld so that he might retrieve her. Yet, her soul never reached the underworld. It had become lost along the way and it could not be found. The man who would become Death grieved all the more and he pledged to himself that never again would a soul be lost on the journey to the underworld. He would escort every one of them, guiding them, so that they would reach the safety of the afterlife. And so he assumed the mantle of the reaper and to this day he escorts the souls of the dead and as he does so he sings his lament, perhaps hoping that the soul of his love will hear it and come to him.'

'Can you sing this lament?' Anna enquired. Gyddyn shook his head.

'I dare not Miss Anna. It is considered to bring ill fortune to those whom it is sung.'

As interesting as this discussion was, and I shan't repeat the lament on these pages for fear of causing offence, Codswallop required my urgent attention.

I entered the drawing room, Gyddyn and Anna in succession behind me. Codswallop was lying on the couch, shaking and holding a bottle of brandy. John Douglas was by his side, holding his hand and watching as he shook. He stood up as I approached.

'Mr Morfas sir. I am glad you have returned. Mr Codswallop is growing weak. I knelt down by the couch and clutched Codswallop's hand.

'Codswallop my dear man. What is wrong? Why did you run across the mountains?'

Codswallop breathed deep before he spoke.

'I followed your instructions sir. Myself and the agents kept watch for the revolutionaries and yesterday we got wind they were housed at an inn in Camberwell. We went there and we watched them and we saw them passing train tickets between themselves... Four of them sir. We didn't know where they were going so this morning we followed them to Euston and to our horror it were the *North Wales Express* which they were boarding.'

'Oh Codswallop! Why ever did you not telegraph?'

'There wasn't time sir. The other agents said they would send a telegram but I didn't have time. I had to get on the train and keep close to them revolutionaries.' I nodded at John Douglas, an indication for him to check to see if any telegrams had arrived for me. Whilst he was gone Codswallop continued to talk.

'I got into their compartment sir. They weren't happy but I got in by pretending there were no other spaces. They spoke in Romanian sir but I heard some familiar names sir. I heard them mention Bethesda and Cythry and Morfasson. They were coming here sir. Where else would they be coming? I don't know how they know but they know where she is. '

'So why didn't you telegraph from the train?' John Douglas now returned, empty handed and I wondered why my men in London had not sent their promised telegram.

'I couldn't telegraph sir. I couldn't leave the compartment. It would have looked odd.'

'So instead you got off at Aber and you ran all the way across the mountains to warn me. You silly, wonderful man Codswallop. You silly, wonderful man!'

'It was the only way sir. It was the only way I could ensure I got here before they did.'

He closed his eyes and said no more, falling instead into a deep sleep.

My first thought was of Anna, who had been petrified.

'Don't let them take me Mr Max… Please! Don't let them

take me!'

'It is quite alright Miss Anna. I shall not let that happen.'

'And neither shall I, Miss Anna the pint,' John Douglas assured.

'And you have the protection of the Dulyn Frodorion,' Gyddyn offered. He then paused and went to look out of the window. 'In fact, if I may suggest it, and this is highly irregular I know, you would be safer in Dulyn than here.'

'Are you saying that my home is not safe?' I was offended by his remark.

'Not in the slightest. But here you are few, there we are many. There are more there who will look out for her safety and guard her.'

'I see your point and it is a wise one. However, what of the omens? What of the damage that taking Anna to Dulyn may cause?'

'I do not like these omens Faban-Morfa. They bode ill for my kin but there are no means by which we shall *prevent* the flow of our blood. If we do nothing for Miss Anna I regret to say that death shall still come for us.'

'Pardon me for saying Mr Gyddyn, but if you take in Miss Anna the pint, would the flow not be worse than otherwise?'

Gyddyn reflected on the words of John Douglas and he paced the room.

'Perhaps. Or perhaps not. Who is to say? If she stays here then shall the bloodshed amongst *your own* people not be worse than otherwise? Whichever path is taken, Death shall sing his lament.'

Anna came from the corner and clung to my shoulders.

'Please Mr Max. I do not wish to die. I am not fond of these people but if the revolutionaries know I am here in the castle then I *shall* be safer in their settlement. I *must* go with this man.'

She was right. I could see the terror in her eyes and I knew that the only way to now protect her was to get her away from the castle, to somewhere she would not be expected. The Dulyn settlement was a first move at least. From there we could plan a further escape.

'If you must go then I shall come with you,' I declared spontaneously. 'I am your assigned guardian and it would not be apt to abandon you at such a moment as when your life is in the most peril. That is, I should come provided that Gyddyn gives his assent.' Gyddyn put a hand over his heart and bowed.

Max & Anna

'You are always welcome in Dulyn, Faban Morfa,' he said.

I looked to John Douglas who was standing, expectantly, awaiting what instructions he knew I should give him.

'John Douglas. You have the management of the estate until such time as I return, as per our usual arrangement. Tell no one where we have gone, not even Belvedere. If you must make contact head for the peak of Llewellyn. A nearby watcher shall then send for me.'

'And of these revolutionaries Mr Morfas sir?'

'Rouse the village. Warn them of the danger. Be wary and do not let the men near if they approach. Do not kill them but do what you must to ward them away.'

I made to leave, taking Anna and Gyddyn with me. Time was of the essence and there was nothing more to be said. John Douglas would do all that needed to be done.

I had gone as far as the door when his voice stopped me.

'Mr Morfas sir...' I turned to see him kneeling by the couch, holding Codswallop by the hand. 'He's dead Mr Morfas sir... Codswallop is dead!'

Alas, the poor man. That run across the mountains in his noble pursuit had exhausted him and pushed his body beyond its natural limits and now that his task was done his heart had surrendered. There was naught we could do for him now but Gyddyn took it upon himself to step forwards and perform a rite which few outside of the Frodorion ever receive. He sang the lament of Death, though only the chorus.

'I thought it brought ill fortune,' Anna whispered in my ear.

'Only if it is sung to a living soul. Then it is seen as a curse. But to sing it to the deceased is a blessing.'

'It is a beautiful blessing,' she said.

-CHAPTER XIV-

Hiding my grief for Codswallop, I took Anna and Gyddyn from the drawing room into the entrance hall and from there led them down deep into the bowels of the castle. Being such an ancient fortress it is, below the level of the ground, peppered with old tunnels and corridors dug for service, subterfuge and storage. Some of those closer to the surface are so large that they are practically caves.

My grandfather[68] was a great enthusiast for 'the under castle', as he called it, and some of the rooms and tunnels near to the surface he had renovated into watertight basement rooms. During the intervening years these have been filled with an assortment of odds, ends, general trash and things that require hiding. Stolen paintings for example.

I had recently adapted one room into an armoury and I made for it, a candle burning in my hand, so that we might have something to defend ourselves with should the need arise. I am not an advocate of guns and I do not like to carry one- I did not even carry one whilst in London or whilst escorting Anna to Cythry. A gun raises questions. It marks a

---

[68] George Morfasson- Born in 1793 and died C.1837

man out, makes people wonder about his need to arm himself. I only use guns, or carry them, when it is an absolute necessity.

'Have you ever fired a gun Miss Anna?' I asked as I removed a flintlock pistol from a case. She took it from me and gave it an examination.

'If you have weapons here, Mr Max, why do we not just gun down the revolutionaries?'

'Because we are not killers Miss Anna,' I scolded. 'We must only use these weapons to defend ourselves and when we have no other option.'

Anna huffed and returned the pistol to me. I placed it into a holster which I attached to my belt and added another pistol of the same design to the opposite side.

'Do not let my people see those Faban-Morfa,' Gyddyn warned.

'Why on earth not?' Anna asked.

'Because to the Frodorion the gun is one of the most evil weapons ever devised. And I agree with them. The *only* reason I am taking these with us is as a very last resort.'

'These guns,' there was distaste in Gyddyn's voice. 'These guns are cruel weapons. They kill in seconds and in numbers that are obscene. One of these could destroy all the hill farmers in a single afternoon. Such weapons offend us.'

'I shall do my best to keep them out of sight,' I promised as we left. I think he understood my reasoning but he was not pleased with it.

'I would prefer that you would not bring them at all. We Frodorion have weapons of our own that you may defend yourself with if the need arises. They are less offensive weapons.' I knew precisely what those weapons were. They were pitchforks and spears and knives, weapons that required combat at close quarters. They would do no good against a group who would themselves be carrying the much despised guns.

I ignored Gyddyn's protest for the reasons I describe above and proceeded to lead my two companions from the basement rooms and down into the depths of the mountain. In the basement rooms the walls are all lime washed and neatened and ordered but the further one goes down the more natural and chaotic things become. There comes a point where one can quite easily become lost if you do not know the way. Even I, who know the undercastle better than anyone, do not know where some of the tunnels lead.

My nanny used to tell me, whenever I was found exploring down there as a child, that one of them went right down into the centre of the earth and that another runs the length of Eryri. Whilst this may not be entirely true some of the tunnels are indeed incredibly deep and I often wonder why some of them were dug in the first place. Some go far beyond what is necessary for service, storage or subterfuge.[69]

The only deep level tunnel which I definitively know the purpose of was the one which we followed. It is known as 'the well' and for centuries it has been used as an escape route. It comes out in the mountainside above Melynlyn, on the far side of Llewelyn, and to get through it is a tricky business. The walls become narrow and in places you have to walk sideways because the tunnel is hardly big enough to accommodate the width of a man. Then there is the part towards the end of the tunnel where the ceiling and the floor are almost one with each other. It comes on in the space of less than a metre and you first find yourself bending slightly

---

[69] It was suggested by Professor Joshua Bandstand in the fifties that the deepest tunnels are the remains of a prehistoric mine, similar to the copper mines on Pen Y Gogarth.

and then dropping to your hands and knees before you are finally forced onto your belly where you must slither the final three hundred metres to the tunnel exit. It was not always this way but years of rain and water have brought debris into the mouth and they have slowly begun to block it up. Due to its infrequent use in modern times it has not been seen as necessary to maintain it.

By this stage in my narrative you can well predict Anna's reaction. You would be right in thinking that she was most aggrieved. What made it worse was that the candle had gone out and I had foolishly brought no matches to replace the flame.

'Mr Max this is intolerable,' she groused when she was forced to her knees by the closeness of the tunnel ceiling. She said the same thing again when she was brought down to her belly. 'Did we really have to come this way?' she added. 'Why could we not have gone *over* the mountains?'

'This way is discreet. Had we gone overland there is every chance that someone may have seen us leaving the castle or crossing the peaks. It is all for your own protection.'

'It is night time Mr Max. No one would have seen us if we went overland without a light.'

'Therein raises another problem Miss Anna. Crossing the mountains at night and without light we may have stumbled over a precipice or fallen foul of a gully.'

'Even we Frodorion, who know the mountains better than any, dare not go out after dark without a light. Ill fortune awaits those who travel the dark.'

Anna grumbled and she continued to crawl forwards.

'I do not like this,' she protested. 'It is most undignified and quite unlady like.'

'Nobody need know what has occurred down here Miss Anna. Gyddyn and I will never tell of your indignity if you choose to forbid such a thing.'

'But what of when you come to write your memoirs Mr Max? How will you tell the story of how you spirited the princess from your castle without expanding on how you thoroughly humiliated her in the process?'

She had a point as things have turned out. In so much as I have thought of neglecting to mention this incident I find that there has been no way to avoid mentioning it. I shall thus keep that mention as brief as I can.

To be fair to Anna slithering through that tunnel *was* a highly unpleasant experience. We could not go back for there was now no way to turn around and to *actually* go back we would have had to slither backwards with no clue as to where in the tunnel we were or how far we would have to continue in such a state. And it seemed like such a long way back to the castle that I could not bear the thought of having to go all that way without light. The thought made the whole undertaking of coming this way seem like such a waste.

At long last I reached the end of the tunnel and I felt fresh air blowing over me. It was a chore to escape as the exit to tunnel is the narrowest part but once I was out these I was relieved to find myself on the shores of Melynlyn, though I could only see a small part of it in the moonlight. I helped Anna out through the hole but Gyddyn would have none of that sort of thing. He valiantly hauled himself through and then he huffed and shook himself.

'I am too old to be crawling on my hands and knees Faban-Morfa. I hope I do not have to traverse that tunnel again.'

'As do I,' Anna snorted petulantly.

Gyddyn took the lead and he guided us along the mountain face to the corner of Melynlyn where he stopped.

'I must tell the village of our approach. I must tell them that I bring outsiders with me.'

Gyddyn raised a hand to his mouth and he made a hollering sound. Seconds later the sound was returned from somewhere in the night. Then he made a different sound and he cocked his ear to listen for a reply. When none was forthcoming he nodded. 'Someone shall be coming to see who you are.'

'I hope they will not be long. I am growing cold,' Anna said.

'I do not wish to be standing around doing nothing when there may be danger afoot,' I added.

'They will not be long,' Gyddyn chided. 'There will be a watcher close and he shall be the one to come.'

From the dark came the bobbing of a safety lamp held high in the hands of a young, long haired Frodorion man. He and Gyddyn bowed their heads to one another.

'Eilio… These are the outsiders,' Gyddyn said in his native tongue. Eilio, who was no more than eighteen or nineteen, came close and shone his light in our faces. He smiled at me and bowed his head.

'Faban-Morfa. It is an honour to have you grace our

farmstead.'

'As I am honoured to be here. May I introduce my companion? This is Miss Anna.' Eilio shone the light in her face for another look and then he took a horrified step backwards.

'She is the lady of blood. She brings death. Why have you brought her here Faban-Morfa?'

'The blood shall flow if she comes or no,' Gyddyn interrupted before I could say anything. 'She has been brought because I have granted her the protection of our people. Evil men stalk this land and she will be safer with us, here, than in the castle.' Eilio sniffed with disgust and he once more shone the light across Anna's face. She did not understand a word of what was being said and her face had the appearance of a lost lamb.

'Very well. But the village shall not like it,' Eilio said.

-CHAPTER XV-

Eilio led us to the Dulyn settlement over some rough, heathery ground that was steep underfoot. We did not see the village until we were right on top of it; a circlet of ten lime washed cottages, no more than two rooms to each building, surrounding a communal square where the Frodorion of Dulyn had gathered to greet us. Each of the buildings had a lit safety lamp hung over the door and the light from them danced across the piazza and reflected in the eyes of the gathered Frodorion.

It was a sight to see, that reflecting light, for all the people had the same amber coloured eyes and the effect created by the light reflecting from so many of them was a thing of mesmeric beauty.[70]

I know of no other people in all the world who are so unreadable as the Frodorion farmer. One can never tell if they will be friendly of hostile. As Anna and I came into the square, following Gyddyn and Eilio, they silently surrounded us to make sure that we could not escape. They

---

[70] The notable and rare amber coloured eyes of the Frodorion farmers is now known to have been a by-product of inbreeding.

held no weapons, weapons are kept secure in the house of the farmstead head, but on the chance that we were a threat they had their own special ways of dealing with us.

'Who comes to Dulyn?' an elderly lady asked in English. She approached forth from the gathered villagers and examined us. She was the oldest woman in the village and thus held in the utmost regard. Her name was Maeneira.

'Faban-Morfa,' she bowed. 'Your presence is an honour. But this lady you bring here to us... This lady courts the reaper. She is not welcome amongst us.' A chorus of 'ayes' filled the air. 'Do you know what we do to unwelcome strangers in these parts? We chase them from our village, oftentimes as far as Bethesda. Are you prepared to run through the night Miss Anna?' Anna trembled before the threat and grabbed my waist for protection.

'She is not an unwelcome stranger,' Gyddyn chastised. 'I have offered her our protection and she shall have it.' Maeneira was incensed and spat on the ground before prowling around the centre of the square, holding the appearance of a poisonous toad.

'She brings death, Gyddyn. Her presence in these parts brings blood. By allowing her into our farmstead you are dooming us all.'

'And yet I may not be. The dreams show that she brings blood to our people… Not in what manner…'

'Her presence here may *be* the reason why our blood shall flow. Did you ponder that leader Gyddyn? Had she not been brought here the dreams may never have come to pass.'

'You know as well as I do, Maeneira, that the visions were too powerful to be averted. Had she come here or no there would be blood.'

Eilio stepped forwards to make his opinions known.

'If I may add to this discussion, leader Gyddyn, elder Maeneira, if we knew *how* she will cause our blood to flow then we might be able to prevent it.'

'Foolish child,' Maeneira snapped. 'How do you propose we learn such a thing? Hope for another dream to show us the way? You know the chances of such a thing are almost zero.'

'True. But as I see it she will be at the centre of the web. She may possess knowledge which we do not.' A murmur of agreement passed from some members of the settlement. Maeneira was not amongst them.

'Go back to your cradle Eilio. We *do not* interpret the

dreams of strangers.'

'And what of Faban-Morfa? He is no stranger and yet he is her protector. He may also hold knowledge that we do not.' Eilio's words chilled Maeneira and she rejected the proposal outright.

'No. Never! To look into the dreams of the Morfa is to stare into the infernal abyss. You know the tale of Mianog as well as any of us.'

To interrupt here, I shall guess that you, dear reader, most likely *do not* know of Mianog. I shall endeavour to explain as best I can. Mianog was the village elder during the time of my twice great grandfather, Eldrick.[71] Eldrick was troubled by recurring nightmares of a disturbing nature. One common one was thus; He saw a wedding in the snow but this scene quickly changed to one of war and bloodshed. He saw the bride and the groom and their assorted wedding guests fighting monstrous beasts before the ground beneath their feet trembled and buckled and ripped apart and all the guests who remained alive were swallowed up by a smoky

---

[71] Little is known of Eldrick except that he was an adventurer and explorer who lived during the 1700s. Some of his papers survive but they have yet to be transcribed.

black maw.

After having this same nightmare each night for a month Eldrick sought the advice of Mianog. Mianog found she could not interpret this nightmare. It was beyond her powers and so, in an effort to learn more of what it signified, she began to ask Eldrick of his other dreams and nightmares, going right back to childhood. Eldrick told and as Mianog listened the collected night time imaginings came together. I know not what she saw within them but they drove her to madness. All she could say forever afterwards was that she had 'seen into the infernal abyss.' Since that day no Frodorion will dare interpret the dreams of a Morfasson, born or by marriage, for fear of that infernal abyss and what they might see within.

Anna had been growing increasingly bewildered for some time owing to the fact that almost all of the discourse was in a language that was alien to her. Now, as Maeneira scolded Eilio for suggesting that my dreams be interpreted, she turned to me.

'What are they saying Mr Max? I do not like it.'

'They are arguing over whether they should interpret your dreams.'

'My dreams? Why ever would they want to know about those?' Gyddyn answered her.

'They may hold the key to understanding from where the blood flow stems, Miss Anna. Eilio argues that if we know that detail we may be able to prevent it.'

'Then I am all for the idea. Especially if it will aid in my protection,' she pompped.

'It is not that simple,' Maeneira blasted. 'We do not interpret the dreams of strangers. Only a child and a fool like Eilio would dare to suggest such a slight against our customs.'

'Then I say it is time you dropped that custom. If it shall help myself then it shall certainly help your people as well. Sometimes it is beneficial to change our habits and this, for you, is one of those times.'

Oh lord! I closed my eyes at the horror of what she had just said, which to a Frodorion I knew would not be acceptable, and I feared the worst. From her wide eyed expression Maeneira was offended and the rest of the village took a step backwards away from us.

'You shall pay for that offence,' she hissed. 'You shall forever be known amongst the Frodorion as Y Lembo

Gwirion... Unwelcome Stranger!'

'No. I have offered her our protection and she will have it. She shall not be named Y Lembo Gwirion whilst I am leader,' Gyddyn intervened.

'And if *you*, Maeneira, shall not be prepared to interpret her dreams for the sake of our protection and hers then I shall,' a woman, middle aged, offered from the crowd. Maeneira turned to the newcomer.

'Are you certain Eirianws? Would you betray the customs of your own kith so readily?'

'I do not see it as the betrayal of our customs, not if it shall benefit us as the lady of death says that it shall.' Maeneira grimaced and looked around, seeing that she was outnumbered and that nobody was prepared to speak up for her.

'Very well then. On your own head be it.'

Maeneira stalked away into the crowd of villagers and was lost to our sight.

Eirianws came forth towards Anna and bowed.

'Miss Anna. If you would accompany me, I shall interpret your dreams.'

'Thank you. May Mr Max come with us? I should feel

more comfortable.'

'It is unusual. Dream interpretation is usually an intimate occasion between two people. However, as we are already breeching custom it shall not harm for him to attend this one time.'

Eirianws took us to one of the cottages and on the way in she removed the safety lamp hanging above the door. Inside the cottage was cramped and the smells of wild foods, fruits and grasses abounded. Salt cured meats hung from the ceiling, mostly freshwater fish but with chevaline and lamb mixed amongst them. There were plenty of chairs upon which to sit and from them we watched as Eirianws used the flame from the safety lamp to light a hearth and bathe the room in a warm flicker. It was a comfortable, humble and homely room.

Eirianws seated herself opposite Anna and first looked over every inch of her face.

'Have you had any sleepless nights of late my child?'

'Only the one. The first night I spent in Mr Max's castle.

'That is good. It means there shall be many fresh dreams to interpret. Hold out your hand child. Faban-Morfa… Could you keep it steady for me?' I lightly held Anna's hand whilst

Eirianws looked over it, without touching. After some minutes she nodded with approval.

'Yes. You have quite the hand Miss Anna. It is very interesting!'

'What does it say?'

'Your life line is in flux so how long you will live I cannot say. Your love line, however, is strong. According to it you are to marry at an age no older than twenty five.' Anna chortled merrily.

'Marry? Can you imagine that Mr Max? What an absurdity this lady presents. I would have to meet a very perfect gentleman before I could even think about marriage.'

'Perhaps you will. I see an enormous change occurring in your life. Such times are usually those when couples come together.'

'Perhaps that change is now, Miss Anna,' I jocularly suggested.

'Do not be so silly Mr Max. I have only met two eligible gentlemen in all my time since leaving Ardeluta. As pretty as he is, I sincerely doubt I would be allowed to marry Eilio. Second is yourself and to marry *you* would be absurd.'

'And why is it such an absurd notion Miss Anna?'

'Because we are not in love with each other for a start. Two people must be in love before they can marry. Secondly my father would never allow such a thing. Thanks to your blasted Queen Victoria you are not nobility and therefore nowhere near eligible enough to marry a princess.'

Her statement hurt me and left me sorrowful but I recovered thanks to an interruption from Eirianws.

'Tell me of your recurring dreams Miss Anna. Have you ever had any?'

'Not as such. But there is always one man whom I see in them. He is always there somewhere.'

'What does he do? Is he good or bad?'

'Good I believe. He assumes different roles, as though he is an actor. Sometimes he is a king and other times he is a soldier. Last night I dreamed I saw him at the opera house in Berlin. On my last night in Paris I dreamed I was attending a ball and he was also there, dancing with a lady.'

'And what does he look like?'

'He is tall and he has deep blue eyes. I always know him by his eyes. He has a beard also.'

'What colour hair has he?' Anna puzzled over this question.

'I do not know the word in English but it is the same colour as old metal. It is a mixture of orange, brown and red.'

'Rust coloured?' I suggested.

'If that is what you would say in English then it almost certainly is.'

'Curious,' Eirianws gasped, frightened. 'Tell me Miss Anna, is this man ever accompanied by others?'

'Always. We are never alone together.'

'Have you ever seen him with a black haired woman, much shorter than himself?'

'Perhaps. I could not say.'

'What of a similar looking man?'

'No. I cannot say that I have. I do not take much notice of the other people in my dreams.'

Eirianws stood and went to the door.

'MAENEIRA!' she called. There was some time of waiting before Maeneira came.

'What is it? What have you seen in the dreams of the stranger?'

'*Him* Maeneira. He is always there.'

'Are the others with him? The black haired woman? The

similar looking man? What of the barbarian?'

'She says that she takes little notice of the others in her dreams.' Maeneira moved in close to Anna, so close that they were only a whisker apart.

'Tell me stranger. What does this man look like?' Anna once again described him, precisely as before. 'And on his finger is there, perchance, a ring banded by a black stone?' Anna looked surprised.

'Why yes! Yes there is!' Maeneira stood firm and cold, still a whisker from Anna's face.

'Then Eirianws must not interpret your dreams any further. We know of this man you dream of. Every once in a while we see him ourselves. We call him Tywyllwch and he is associated with the infernal abyss.[72] To stare any deeper into your dreams, therefore, would be to risk absolute madness.' She finally moved away, back towards the door. 'Sleep now. Sleep in this house and dream once more of Tywyllwch. Eirianws and I must talk.'

When we were alone by the flickering fire Anna took hold of my arm.

'Mr Max I am worried. What is this infernal abyss of

---

[72] Tywyllwch means 'Darkness.'

which the old woman speaks?'

'I do not know much of it Miss Anna. I have heard the Frodorion mention it before now but only in one context. I have only heard it mentioned when concerning the dreams of my family, the dreams of the Morfasson.'

-CHAPTER XVI-

Faith and religion are deep rooted aspects of the Cymric psyche, especially in the north. We are a devout people and everyone you meet shall have a religion of one kind or another. For the most part it is Christianity that dominates, in particular Presbyterian Christianity. You will see the evidence of this in every town and every village you visit. Each of them will have at least one church or chapel and the most common types are square, none-descript buildings without feature or ornamentation. Only in the very smallest of hamlets, like Cythry or Pen Y Gwryd, will you find no such building.

At Cythry our nearest church is on the Ogwen road, short of Capel Curig, and the residents of that village are more than pleased to accept us as a part of their congregation. As almost all residents of Cythry are Christian each week Evans the horse readies a special cart and escorts a number of the residents to the church. He cannot fit the entire village and so those who take the cart are often those who are unable or too old to walk the distance to Capel Curig. However, when the weather is particularly bad, when it rains in sheets rather than droplets, or when the snow is thick on the ground, Evans fits a canvas awning and he will make several trips between Capel Curig and Cythry so that nobody will have their Sunday best ruined. I have a photograph, somewhere, of this cart and all the people piled inside whilst bedecked in their finest. It is a lovely picture but I cannot include it here owing to publishing costs.

I am not religious myself, though I believe there must be some purpose to life and a higher power overseeing it all. I believe there is more than the world we see. There is more than the short life we live and what lies beyond our perceptions is both unknowable and glorious. I am not certain that the Christian belief is the correct one but I do join the other villagers in the church at Capel Curig when I can and I also attend the Easter services at Bangor Cathedral as well as the Christmas services when the winter weather allows.

I often find the sermons of a cleric, any cleric, whatever their religion, to be worth listening to. Even if one does not agree there shall always be something to contemplate or reflect upon. The sermons of clerics are often wise and learned and our reactions to them tell us a great deal about ourselves.

It is in the larger settlements of North Wales where you will find many of the non-Presbyterian faiths. Both Bangor and Bethesda have innumerable churches, as do Conwy and Caernarfon. Bangor, as well as having its fine but small cathedral, is the home to several convents as well as a modest synagogue.[73] I hear of plans afoot to construct a mosque in the city but I doubt that these will come to much as whilst there *is* an Islamic population in the region there are not enough worshippers, at present, to warrant the cost of construction.[74]

There are no Catholic churches in the area[75] but it is well worth noting that some of the most prominent people in the region are, in fact, followers of that religion. I previously mentioned, in passing, Monsignor Hywell, but the warden of Caernarfon Gaol and the school master at Llanberis are two other examples. The most famous, however, is the Baron Penrhyn. His faith is one of the few things which I

---

[73] This was known as the Bangor Hebrew Congregation- I cannot find where it was precisely but it was located in the 'Arvonia Buildings' on the High Street. It closed at some point after 1947.

[74] Today there is a mosque in Bangor- The Bangor Islamic Centre- Located towards the end of the High Street.

[75] This is no longer true.

admire him for and neither he, nor his predecessors, have ever been ashamed to admit their allegiance. Penrhyn Castle is stuffed to the gills with catholic imagery and it even houses a chapel which is by far the greatest part of the whole structure.

You may be wondering why I have bothered to describe this in such detail. I do so because the next day was Sunday and the Frodorion are some of the most devout people in all the region. They may have a particular set of ideas and superstitions concerning life, culture and death but at their heart they are a Christian people. They believe in Jesus Christ and the holy trinity and they observe the laws of the Abrahamic god. They take the Sabbath very seriously and as their guests both Anna and myself were expected to obey it also.

We were awoken at dawn by Eirianws. Having not slept a great deal we were both grouchy. Anna was grumpier than I and was all prepared to protest the awakening and surely would have done had I not persuaded her that it would deeply offend our hosts if she did. Her response was stony silence and within it she could have gone either way but she chose the more sensible of the two options in the end, thank

Max & Anna

goodness.

She was again aggrieved soon after when she learned that there was to be no breakfast until after morning worship had been completed. At this she was outraged and kicked up an enormous fuss, first railing against Eirianws.

'This is intolerable. How is a lady supposed to pray upon an empty stomach?'

'With ease Miss Anna. You shall be given no food until after morning prayers have been completed,' Eirianws scolded.

'Then I shall take the matter up with Mr Gyddyn.'

Before I could protest at her rudeness and before Eirianws could tell her that taking it up with Gyddyn would have little impact she had marched from the cottage, wearing a night gown borrowed from a similar sized Frodorion lady I should hasten to add, and was loudly demanding that she speak to Gyddyn at once. He was across the pizza in conversation of the hushed variety with Maeneira. Anna behaved as rudely as was possible and she barged right into their conversation.

'Mr Gyddyn. I demand that I be given some food this instant.'

'That is not how we do things Miss Anna. We do not eat on

a Sunday until we have reaffirmed our commitments to God and to Christ.'

'I do not care if it is how you do things. If you *will not* give me food then find it elsewhere.'

'And where should that be Miss Anna?' Maeneira cackled. 'You cannot climb the mountains and return all the way to Cythry on an empty stomach. If you go by any low land route then it is a fair way to the next place where you might find food.'

Anna was cowed into silence by these words and she returned to the cottage with a furious expression. She then pouted at the cured meats hanging from the ceiling for half an hour until the time came for morning worship.

This began with prayers in the piazza, led by Gyddyn, and they were followed by a procession from the settlement up to Llyn Dulyn. That lake is black, made blacker by walls of hard rock that surround it and overshadow it on three sides. On one edge, partially built into the cliffs, is a tower, Castell Dulyn.[76] It comprises only of a squat, round building and is

---

[76] The tower was completely destroyed during the last year of the Second World War after Polish troops stationed in the area used it for target practice.

anchored into the rock by flying buttresses. It is one of the few surviving pre-conquest Welsh defensive structures in the north and apart from the roof and the interior floors and walls it is almost the same as it was when originally constructed by Llewellyn Fawr.

The Frodorion like to claim that it was built by God at the time of creation but this is certainly not true, although it does look to be the case I shall admit. Not much is known of why it was constructed nor why it was built so close to a Frodorion settlement. I suppose that in those days there were a great many more of those settlements around than there are today so it was probably the case that *every* castle and defensive tower was close to a Frodorion settlement.

In the shadow of this tower and by the shores of that lake, a sermon was delivered. It concerned Jonah and his trials. The main point of the sermon was to argue that it was not the place of man to decide who should be punished but the choice of God and God alone. Jonah's trials, such as being swallowed by the whale, whom the Frodorion call Rhymynydd, were because he would not go to Nineveh and warn them of God's impending punishment if they did not change. It was solely for the reason that he thought they *should* be punished and Jonah felt that God *should* punish them anyway and not give them a get-out clause. He, Jonah, was punished by God for making his own decision on the punishment. It transpired that the sermon was given, unusually it was an entirely English sermon, for the benefit of myself and Anna.

'I hope you enjoyed my sermon, Faban-Morfa,' Gyddyn said as we returned to the settlement. 'The story of Jonah is one of the favourites amongst my people.'

'You certainly presented an interesting argument,' I replied.

'Yes. Only God should punish the wicked and the evil. Only God can punish. I must be honest with you Faban-Morfa. I was hoping that the sermon would force you to reflect on how you intend to deal with these revolutionaries.'

'I have no intention of *killing* them or doing anything violent if that is your meaning.'

'That I understand, but what you must learn is that you must deal with them without punishing them for their sins. That, only God may do.'

'And what of Miss Anna? Must she not have her desserts for what these men have done to her family?'

'No she must not. Above all else she must forgive them,

Max & Anna

and in years to come she may thank them. But she *must not* punish them. They are not the only ones she mustn't punish... The Baron Penrhyn, for example?'

'You know of that?'

'Naturally. We have received wind of stolen paintings and we also saw Miss Anna and Evans the horse riding a loaded cart along the Ogwen road. It was not difficult to understand. She stole those paintings as a result of hearing tales of the baron's less redeeming qualities, did she not?'

'Indeed she did.'

'At least, therefore, it was for no personal reason and God may yet forgive her. There must be no more punishments.'

I planned to speak to Anna on the matter, yet at that precise moment she had marched on ahead, hoping to get her long desired for breakfast as soon as possible. She was in for a shock as the Frodorion eat as a community upon a Sunday and she would not receive any food until everyone was seated. I imagined that when she learned of this she would stamp her feet and demand that she be fed at once. She acted in quite the opposite way, however. She arrived shortly behind two young women, of whom she asked where she might find food, and was given the response that she would have to wait until the village was gathered and prepared for the occasion. For the sole reason that she might receive her long desired breakfast all the sooner she threw herself into those aforementioned preparations.

She helped to bring chairs and tables out from the cottages and she was instrumental in the erection of a large awning under which all would sit and eat. We were grateful for it as the sky was darkening and very soon it would rain. Lastly Anna was at the head of the group which brought out the food. It had all been prepared the previous evening, so as not to profane the Sabbath; a breakfast of cold meats, some of them cured, and hard boiled eggs and bowls of salad and some candied fruits thrown in for good measure. All of it was simple food grown and prepared around the settlement of Dulyn. We are so spoilt in the modern age that our food can come from anywhere, from as far afield as Spain would you believe, so it is nice to be reminded, every once in a moon, of the foods which may be found on our doorsteps.[77]

We began to eat, after a prayer of thanks, and Anna was the first to dive for the food. The Frodorion do not use

---

[77] As I am sure we all know this statement is nothing when compared to the modern era where food really *can* come from anywhere.

cutlery but this did not bother Anna. She just filled as much of her plate with food as she could and then began to shovel it into her mouth by the handful. This was one of the most uncivilized things which I ever saw her do.

It was only after the food and when we were alone together in Eirianws's cottage that I was able to talk to her of the sermon.

'What did you think of it?'

'I liked how Mr Gyddyn delivered it in English. That was for our benefit, yes?'

'More for your benefit than mine Miss Anna. I can understand the Frodorion tongue quite well, as you know. What did you think of the theme?'

'Jonah? I never understood that story. Why did God not have the man washed upon the nearest shore rather than go through all the hoo ha of involving a whale?'

'Had Jonah merely been washed ashore it would not have been such a trial. He may not have known he was being punished for disobeying God.'

'Perhaps. But why a whale? Surely a shark would be more terrifying and would be more likely to terrify him into obedience.'

'God is not so cruel as all that Miss Anna. He is more subtle and does not, to my knowledge, resort to 'scaring' people into obedience.'

'Then why threaten the Assyrians with fire and damnation? Surely that was scaring them into obedience?'

'I believe you miss the point of the story Miss Anna. As Gyddyn argued so well, the point of the story is to explain that it is not for man to punish, or to decide who is punished, but rather only God himself.'

'I suppose that applies to ourselves? I suppose it is not our prerogative to punish the revolutionaries for what they have done, for pursuing me half way across the continent? I say it is all pish and nonsense. If *we* are not to punish them then where is their punishment from God? Why have they not yet been punished? Answer me that, Mr Max.'

'Perhaps it shall come many years in the future.'

Anna cackled as if she were drunk.

'Or perhaps not. And besides which... Have they themselves not already broken this deific decree? Have they not broken it by attempting to punish my family for our sins against Ardeluta? If they have breached the law of God then surely they should have been punished as Jonah was punished for *his* disobedience of the same decree.'

'Perhaps…'

'You start so many sentences with 'perhaps' Mr Max. I say that perhaps they are not going to be punished at all.'

'I was going to say, Miss Anna, that they may yet be punished on the day of judgement.'

'And by then it will be too late. What would be the point? Punishment should come as an immediate consequence of a bad action. It should not be delayed or what is the use? A man must have the opportunity to learn from his mistakes. By God's method there is little chance of wrong doers learning from their mistakes. Man *must* punish as God will not do it in a sufficient enough manner by himself.'

The conversation travelled in circles from that point on, until I realized that she was not going to listen to reason.

Now that I look back I am not surprised that she took the position which she did. If it had been my own family who were wronged I would wish for the perpetrators to face swift punishment. I would not leave such a thing in God's hands alone.

-CHAPTER XVII-

Towards midday John Douglas was sighted atop Llewellyn. I could not have spotted him myself as the clouds over the mountaintops gave hardly an inch of the peaks to be viewed. They were thick, dense and grey, producing the kind of rain that falls in sheets rather than droplets. It was Eilio who had sighted him.

As I stepped outside I was soaked to the bone in a matter of five seconds. I was aghast and astounded.

'Eilio,' I cried over the sound of the rain thrumming off the ground and off the rooftops of the cottages. 'Eilio, how on earth could you see him in this weather?'

'With a lifetime of practice Faban-Morfa,' was his only response. They were the last words I heard spoken until I reached John Douglas.

It was to be a hellish chore getting to him and I soon cursed the fact that he had chosen such weather to come see me. I hoped that it was for a damn good reason.

Eilio began by leading me back towards Llyn Dulyn where now the way had become boggy under foot. Eilio barely ever touched the ground but with each step *I* took my boots were sucked into the earth, caking the bottom of my trousers in mud. I had to use all my strength to get them free. It slowed our progress and by the time we reached the lake both Eilio and myself were tired of it. Those boots sticking in the mud were slowing us down and so I signalled to Eilio that I wished to make a detour in order to temporarily dispose of them.

I should recommend to anyone that if they are ever to be required to walk over boggy ground, through a rainstorm as I had to do that you remove your footwear and go barefoot. The human foot is a miracle of nature and it is a shame to continuously encase it in layers of cotton and leather as we do. The foot has evolved to carry a man about the earth and across any terrain and is perfectly suited to doing so. This especially includes boggy terrain and once I was barefoot then I no longer sank into the mud, which had something to do with surface area and the spread of a barefoot foot being less evenly distributed than the flat of a shoe. With the weight being less spread there was less pressure upon the mud. At least that is if I am not mistaken.

Leaving my boots, soaked and covered with mud, beneath

an overhang of Castell Dulyn we continued on to the back of the lake and to where the waters came closest to lapping up against the mountains. It could hardly be seen in all the rain but there was a path snaking and winding up through the rocks of the cliff and up towards the slopes of Foel Grach. I was even more glad now that I had ditched my boots as up here they would not have supported me or given me sufficient grip. The boggy ground of the track up to the lake gave way gave way to slippery, slimy, solid earth; not rock but not quite mud either. It was somewhere between the two. It became more rocky the further we travelled up the mountain and it was pure rock on either side of the path but for our climb we had to endure that middle type of ground beneath our feet.

That path was steep and both myself and Eilio used every ounce of our climbing skill to fight against the weather and reach the top. It required balance to stay upright and on the surface of the path and we had to grab hold of whichever rain sodden rock we could get our hands on in order to remain steady and to haul ourselves to the top of the path. I again cursed John Douglas for choosing a day like this to come and speak to me.

Once at the top and on the slopes of Foel Grach the going was easier and more gentle but thanks to the rain it took a great deal longer than it ought to have done to reach the peak Llewellyn.

The weather situation had grown worse the further we climbed and now my main thoughts, besides how terrible an idea this trek was, was that we were taking so long and the weather was so poor that John Douglas might give up hope of speaking to me and return to Cythry. I began to believe that Eilio and I were undertaking this ordeal for no good purpose.

But no.

John Douglas was still very much there, standing at the top of the mountain and holding a pink umbrella over his head. He was as still as a post and was far too comical a sight to be laughed at. Had someone cast a six foot five statue in bronze and hauled it all the way up here? Why on earth anyone would wish to place any statue in such a ridiculous place is beyond me but that is much the impression I got when I saw John Douglas standing there atop the mountain.

He saw us approach and with a smile he came to cover me

with his umbrella. It was heaven to be out of the rain at last but there was little room underneath the thing and I had to get far too intimate with John Douglas. I recall, and it was the first and only time I ever noted this, that there was an odour of chamomile about him, ever so slightly feminine.

'John you accursed man, you'll catch your death coming up here in this weather. What am I saying? I'll catch *my* death coming up here in this weather!'

'I'm sorry Mr Morfas but I wouldn't have come if it wasn't important. You recall those paintings Miss Anna stole from the Baron Penrhyn? He's come up from London and he's fuming about them.'

'I expected he might be. How is this of any importance John?'

'He wants them back real bad. Beddgelert has got wind that the baron has called in soldiers from Chester to come find them.'

'The army? Why on earth is he not using the police?'

'Beddgelert isn't sure but he believes it is because the baron thinks he will get better results with the soldiers.' I grumbled at the news. The last thing we needed was a bunch of English soldiers wandering about the place, antagonising the local population as English soldiers always do.

'What news is there of the revolutionaries?' I asked, looking out beyond the mountain where I could see nothing but cloud and rain.

'They're staying at the Illyrian in Bethesda but we haven't learned more than that.'

That they were staying in the Illyrian made perfect sense now that I heard it. It was the dirtiest, most foul and seediest club in Bethesda and if ever a man wanted to mingle with the lowest forms of humanity possible then that was where he should seek them.

'We must keep an eye on them. See what they do and where they go,' I proposed. 'You have sent men to the place already, yes?'

'Certainly Mr Morfas. It is my reckoning that they will first make for Cythry, attempt a direct assault on Miss Anna.'

'Yes. Without a shadow of a doubt. The question is which route will they take? They might attack by the Ogwen road or they could cross the mountains in an attempt to catch us unawares. The Ogwen road is the more likely, especially in this weather.' John Douglas disagreed, shaking his head.

'I would not put it past them to try the mountain route Mr

Morfas. All they would need was a guide and there are many in Bethesda who would take on such a job for the money. And if SHEMBLE are still backing them then they'll have plenty of that at their disposal.'

He made a good point. All it *would* take was a guide and it wouldn't be hard for a person to convince them that the mountain route to Cythry was sometimes faster and easier than following the Ogwen road. Almost anyone in Bethesda was capable of convincing them of *that*.

'We must find a way to stop these men where they stand John. We must find a way to stop their madness but it must *not* be violent. It would not be fitting for us to be violent.'

'We could try talking to them Mr Morfas,' John Douglas grinned.

'They are not the sort of men who will listen to reason…' I spoke first before thinking of his suggestion. 'But sometimes the ideas we think will not work are the ones that work the best. Tell you what John… Send a diplomat to the Illyrian. Have them attempt to convince the revolutionaries to return home to Romania. Convince them their vendetta is futile. It is a shot in the dark but any shot is worth taking.'

'I will send someone as soon as I return to the castle. Do

you have any further instructions Mr Morfas?'

'Keep a watch on the Ogwen road. I will have the Frodorion keep a watch on the mountains. Should the revolutionaries happen to come to Cythry send for me right away.'

Again, John Douglas bowed and without so much as a goodbye he departed, taking his pink umbrella with him and casting me back under the showers.

-CHAPTER XVIII-

'English Soldiers? Here? I do not like it!' Gyddyn paced around Eirianws's cottage and trembled more than I was. I had not felt the full effects of the rain until I had returned to the village, drenched to the quick, and sat down before the fire. Five minutes and one report of news later I was shivering beneath a moth eaten blanket before that same said fire and with a wooden cup of warm milk between my hands. Besides myself and Gyddyn, Eilio, Maeneira and Anna were present.

'Why use *English* soldiers? Is there not a garrison at Caernarfon?' Eilio asked.

'There is indeed,' Maeneira sneered.

'It is Penrhyn's contempt for the Welsh people,' Anna barged indignantly. 'He does not believe that the Welsh soldiers will do a decent job, clearly.'

'Or it may be that he suspects my involvement,' I guessed. 'He may have chosen to use soldiers from Chester as I have no influence over them. Caernarfon barracks has always been patronized by my family you see. Penrhyn knows that if they were to discover any involvement I had in the theft I could easily turn them away from the truth. He would not get the result he was after.'

'*Any* soldiers in these mountains would be a bad thing,' Gyddyn snapped. 'By their nature they are men of death and destruction. I will admit the Caernarfon soldiers would be preferable to English soldiers but I would still not be pleased by their presence.'

'Could we not negate them by the simple return of the paintings?' Eilio suggested.

'No. Fool of a boy,' Maeneira snagged. I was far gentler with my response.

'This is the *Baron Penrhyn* of whom we talk Eilio. Returning the paintings at this stage would do little good. We cannot hand Miss Anna to him. He would chain her up for the remainder of her days so it would have to be done anonymously. Then he would still hunt for her and the soldiers would crawl over this countryside regardless.'

The silence which followed was broken by a naïve question from Anna.

'If these men are soldiers could we not work with them to combat the revolutionaries?'

'No Miss Anna. Penrhyn will have selected the most

dedicated men for the task. They will have no interest in our revolutionaries, only the recovery of the paintings.'

'And what of this other garrison? This garrison at Caernarfon?'

'They could do no more than my own men are currently doing.'

'Not to mention that we *do not* like soldiers in these parts,' Maeneira rasped. 'Had Faban-Morfa called in soldiers he would no longer be welcome amongst the Frodorion peoples.'

Gyddyn stopped before the fire, knelt down and looked into it. He blew on the flames and then toasted his hands against them a while. In the flickering light his amber eyes looked worn and heavy. He looked to be a very sad and miserable man at that moment.

'I am afraid,' he said quietly.

'Of what Mr Gyddyn?' Anna asked.

'Of everything you have brought to these mountains Miss Anna. First the revolutionaries and now these soldiers who come to find the paintings you stole. I am afraid of the death which you bring us. Most of all I am afraid of what may lie within your soul. You are connected with the infernal abyss.'

Anna was humbled into concern by his fears.

'If you wish me to leave I shall do so, Mr Gyddyn.'

'It is not so simple as all that Miss Anna. The revolutionaries are already here. The soldiers are coming. Your leaving would change nothing. Besides which, it is not safe.'

A pause passed between the three Frodorion in the room. Events were challenging their way of life and their faith to the limits. Anna appeared at her most humble, sorrowed by Gyddyn's fears and worried that she had done something terrible. I was completely adrift. I knew not what to do about the revolutionaries or the coming of the soldiers. Anna was depending upon me for protection but I also had to keep the people with whom I shared my home in mind as well. I could not offend them. I did not know what to do.

No more was said and soon the three Frodorion had departed for their own cottages, leaving Anna and myself alone together and to discuss matters. Anna moved from where she was sat across the room and pulled a chair up next to me, sitting down and placing her head upon my shoulder. By instinct I began stroking her hair.

'I have upset everyone.'

'Through no fault of your own,' I soothed. 'You were not to know that Penrhyn would call upon English soldiers to retrieve his paintings. And you cannot, no matter what the Frodorion may say, control your dreams.'

'Perhaps,' she smiled briefly and then diverted.

'When *I* was upset as a child my father would always sing to me. He sang a song about the sun and how when it goes away it always returns. I wish he were here to sing it to everyone now.'

'I know of a similar song my own father used to sing. I should sing it to you if you like.'

'Would you Mr Max? I would love to hear it. It would brighten me a great deal.'

I straightened my back, puffed out my chest and then began to sing.

The sun has gone,
Away, away,
Far away,
Today, today.
Beyond the trees and 'cross the seas,
The sun has gone away today.

But never fear,
My dear, my dear,
He will return,
Some day, some day.
From 'cross the seas and beyond the trees,
He will return some day, my dear.

When I had done Anna was staring at me, bright eyed and alive with wonder.

'Thank you Mr Max. That *has* brightened me. You have a lovely singing voice. Perhaps if you sung to the Frodorion it would brighten them also.' I chuckled to myself, momentarily.

'Perhaps it would. They do enjoy their music though usually they reserve it for significant occasions... A birth or a death or such things' Anna's head nuzzled my shoulder.

'I like how in the song you referred to me as 'your dear,' Mr Max.'

'They were only the lyrics of the song Miss Anna,' I hastened.

'Of course. But I still liked being your dear all the same.

May I be your dear?' I pulled away from her.

'Miss Anna that would not be appropriate.'

It was an excuse more than any genuine reason.

'Of course it shall be appropriate Mr Max. Why would it not be? I shall be your dear and you shall be my... Well I have not yet decided what you shall be but you shall be my something.'

I let her girlish idea fall by the wayside and returned her to the more pressing matter.

'We really *must* come up with a solution to derail these revolutionaries and English soldiers.'

Anna spread herself across my lap in a scandalously intimate manner. It made me most uncomfortable. What would have happened had one of the Frodorion walked in? That sort of behaviour is most disapproved of. Golly, had we been *anywhere* and someone had walked in on us that behaviour would have been most disapproved of. Anna did not care despite my protestations.

'A nanny of mine used to say that where it is at all possible you should always opt to kill as many birds with a single stone. Perhaps that is how we should deal with the soldiers and the revolutionaries.'

Max & Anna

'If only there were such a way Miss Anna,' I mourned. Anna made herself further comfortable on my lap.

'The soldiers look for the paintings, yes?'

'Yes. And those paintings are currently in one of my cellars!'

'What if they were not? What if they were instead in the hands of the revolutionaries?'

The idea electrified me. I, gently, removed Anna from her scandalous position on my lap and ran to make the suggestion to Gyddyn. I must have knocked on the door of every cottage to find him, and it was still raining. When I succeeded he was still morose but after I told of the idea to place the stolen paintings with the revolutionaries he began to dance about the cottage.

'Faban-Morfa this is marvellous. It is a peaceful solution, for *our* actions anyhow, and that is the most important thing. All necessary parties are appeased. The English soldiers shall no longer have business here, the revolutionaries shall be dealt with and Baron Penrhyn shall have his paintings returned. Best of all there shall be no bloodshed.'

I have never seen any man so excited as Gyddyn was at that moment but now I can only look back in sorrow, knowing as I do of what sadness was to follow.

-CHAPTER IXX-

At dawn the village was aroused by a cry so terrible and so filled with grief that none could fail to investigate what had caused it. Eirianws, Anna and myself came out into the square, all in our nightclothes and still confused by sleep, and we saw a woman on the ground weeping buckets of tears. I knew that she was not of Dulyn as I did not recall seeing her before that morning. I should have recognized her had she been a Dulyn Frodorion. A striking lady of middle age.

It broke me to see a lady in such distress and I wished that I could break the customs of the Frodorion and go to her and hold her as she deserved, to ask her what the matter was.

Fortunately for myself the Frodorion *will* break their own customs when such times demand it so I was not destined to be left helpless for long. Maeneira, the most traditionally entrenched of all, placed a tender and aged hand on the lady's cheek, which she (the lady) held against it.

'My child,' Maeneira soothed with a kindly voice. She needed to say no more.

'Men... Villainous men who spoke neither English nor

Welsh.'

My heart went to my mouth. There was only one group she could be referring to and I feared that they had reached a new and terrible low in their quest for vengeance. Anna, despite not understanding what was said, somehow also knew who she was referring to. She came close to my side and I put a protective arm around her.

'What did these men do my child?' The lady could hardly respond for want of breath between her sobs.

'They came in the dead of night and they raided our village with weapons… Evil weapons. Guns! They kept shouting the same thing at us, over and over again… Printesa.'

'Princess!' I heard Anna gulp beneath her breath.

'The men folk started to fight back but they were no match for them. They shot every last man dead and then they invaded our homes. They tore them apart, all the time shouting 'Printesa' in such an angry way. They were searching for someone. Anyone who tried to stop them was killed. My sister's girl Bronydd was cut down when she tried to fight them off. I managed to escape but not before they started to do terrible things to those who remained alive.'

Maeneira took her hand from the cheek of the lady and let her fall into her arms, where she continued to weep, before starting to lead her to somewhere more private.

I still had my arm protecting Anna when Gyddyn came to talk to me.

'The lady is of the High Rachub village,[78] Faban-Morfa,' he said.

'Closest to Bethesda… They are searching all the villages for our princess,' I spoke so that Anna could not understand me and become alarmed.

'Indeed. Somehow they *know* she is not at Cythry and it seems that they have become so desperate that they are willing to perform great evils to find her. We must go to High Rachub at once."

'And Miss Anna?' I was worried about leaving her at such a time as this.

'She will be safe in the care of Maeneira and Eirianws.'

I bowed my understanding and turned to Anna.

'I must go… But only for an hour or so.'

'It *is* the revolutionaries, yes?' She sounded very

---

[78] High Rachub should not be confused with the nearby and similarly named village of Rachub.

frightened. Her voice quavered and her lips trembled as she spoke.

'Yes. You will be safe here for now. I shall not be long.' Anna smiled, though still showing she was afraid, and then kissed my cheek.

'Please take care Mr Max.'

'I shall,' I promised before we parted.

Gyddyn and I, alongside Eilio and another man called Taicochion, walked up to the mountain plains and there I witnessed an extraordinary sight. It was the capture of two wild horses for our journey to High Rachub. Not so long ago I had the chance to see Buffalo Bill's Wild West show and it was much of a similar thing.[79] Taicochion and Gyddyn transformed two ropes into a lasso and each cast one about the neck of a wild horse. The horses struggled against their captivity but only until Gyddyn and Taicochion could reel them close and soothe them.

The Frodorion are not skilled horsemen, although they know how to ride and they know how to catch the wild horses so that they might tend to them as needed, or when needing to cross the mountains in a hurry.

---

[79] This was in 1904.

Max & Anna

With two of us per horse, Gyddyn and Taicochion on one and myself and Eilio on another, we rode out across the mountains to High Rachub. I think Eilio was unsure about riding with me. I could feel him shifting about in discomfort after he was seated and whilst we were riding he did his best not to touch me, although there was little else to hold onto *except* myself. He attempted to hold his arms around my waist without contact, his hands resting about a centimetre from the front of my chest, but I was too large a man for him to be able achieve it successfully.

We rode, bareback, right across the plains as fast as we could. As I was the most accomplished rider Eilio and I soon took the lead, crossing over Uchaf and Yr Aryg and then between Bera Mawr and Bera Bach. As we came to Drosgl we were met by an unholy sight. Before us lay the three low hills of Gyrn, Llefn and Moel Faban and from the slopes of Moel Faban arose dirty black plumes of smoke, thicker than any that ever rose from the Penrhyn Slate Quarry. Smoke meant fire and we rode towards it at a faster pace.

High Rachub had been the same as Dulyn village except that it was in a more exposed position and there was a well in the centre of the square. Coming upon it we saw the place was an inferno, every one of the cottages alight and roaring orange. Bravely battling this fire with futility and water from the well were Frodorion men and boys from other villages. I recognized some as leaders; Meibion of Llanllechid[80], Ywda of Llefn and Caseg of Wigau. Their presence gave me hope. They signaled that, as yet, this was the only village assaulted by the revolutionaries.

Meibion saw us arrive and left off supervising the fire fighting.

'Leader Gyddyn... Faban-Morfa.' He did not greet Eilio or Taicochion by name but he bowed to them all the same. 'I am glad you have come... Something terrible has happened here.' Gyddyn explained what we knew.

'The lady of blood? So it is true, Faban-Morfa? You have brought her to Cythry?'

'As of this moment she is in Dulyn, where she is hopefully safe. I shall explain all when our work placating the fire has been done.'

It was a tough inferno to fight. It took much of the

---

[80]Tthe Frodorion village of Llanllechid, which as with High Rachub should not be confused with the non-Frodor settlement of the same name.

morning. The only water available was water from the well and we had but one small pale to raise it. People from lower Llanllechid and Bethesda and Rachub climbed Moel Faban to help but there was little they could do. Those that stayed stood in respectful silence and watched as the village burned and the fire was fought as much as it were possible to fight it. It was probably the first and only time many of them had set foot in a Frodorion village but at such a time their concern and their presence and what little aid they gave was most welcome. In the end the fire burned itself out, leaving a black, ashen scar on the side of Moel Faban.

Then came the awful task of learning what had become of the villagers.

The only soul of High Rachub who had been seen that day was the lady who came to Dulyn and by instinct we knew that all the others must be dead. Everybody present assisted in the search for their remains, sifting through the ashes and the rubble of the cottages. It did not take long to discover them. They had been piled, haphazardly and disrespectfully, one atop the other, inside one of the cottages. I do not know how many of them had still been alive when the fire started but surely some of them, I thought, must have been. All the bodies had been charred beyond recognition.

I hope never in all my remaining days to see such a sight again and I pray that nobody reading this volume has to witness such a sight either.

The Frodorion did not hesitate to begin putting their slain brethren to rest. I and the other non-Frodor peoples present dug a deep trench and with all of us working at it the task did not take long. In the meantime all of the bodies were carefully and tenderly, delicately, brought forth from the remains of the cottage and laid out in the square. Some were only children and one, a mere babe, crumbled to dust in the arms of the man who carried him. The distress caused by this occurrence was evidenced by the silent tears that streaked his face.

When all this was done the leaders who were present gave prayers for the departed and each person was laid to rest in the trench before being covered over with a fine layer of soil. When all were laid the remainder of the mass grave was filled and those once good and innocent people were returned to the earth the song of the departed began, sung in its entirety. It was begun by Ywda alone but then the other leaders joined in and then all the remainder of the Frodorion and then the men of Bethesda and its outlying villages and myself joined in with them. Our voices echoed across the mountains to the neighbouring villages and they too joined in the singing. It reached the ears of all at large on the plains, the watchers and those out gathering food or enjoying the morning. They, instinctively knowing a great tragedy had occurred, joined with the singing. Miraculously it reached Dulyn and the village at Llyn Eigiau and they too partook. It was even caught by the residents of Cythry, who I am proud to say sang also. Even across the far side of the Bethesda valley in the Penrhyn Slate Quarry, I am told that all the workers downed tools and sang the song in full. The mountains reverberated to the sound of music and all who heard it knew that the farmers were a people in mourning and many, though they did not yet know the reason why, grieved alongside them.

When the mountains fell silent the men of Bethesda and Llanllechid and Rachub returned to their homes and the Frodorion held council.

I stayed away from this council and instead climbed to the top of Moel Faban. I was covered by dirt and grime and ash, still in my nightclothes, and I longed to fall into a violent rage. The people of High Rachub were innocent, some of them only children for Christ's sake, but the revolutionaries had become so desperate for their revenge that they no longer cared who else they destroyed in the process. In one way, though this may not have been intentional, it was a warning to all the peoples of the area- Surrender the princess or you too shall suffer this fate. I hated them for that, hated them for daring to perform such wicked acts upon my homeland. I did not cry, the tears would come some days following, but I brooded and thought of all the nasty, vile punishments which I could inflict upon the perpetrators of this evil.

Somewhere in my heart I knew that it was not my place to inflict such punishments upon them, that if I tortured and mutilated them I would be no better than they were. I should take a leaf from the Frodorion. They would not be seeking revenge or punishment for this despite its terrible awfulness. They would be following the lessons of Jonah and leaving both the judgement and the punishment in the hands of God. A good man would do as they would. A good man would forgive their evils and leave their fate in the hands of God.

I could not allow them to take any more innocent lives.

Max & Anna

They had to be removed from the land and set aside from their heinous task. Could that still be done in a peaceful way after all this? Yes... I eventually supposed that it *could*. Planting the stolen paintings upon them and pointing the approaching soldiers in their direction would take them out from beneath our feet and it would be, with luck, an entirely bloodless action. They would be escorted to Caernarfon to await trial and then they would face a form of justice. It could never be proven that they were the ones behind the massacre, so their sentence would never be capital one, but Penrhyn would ensure that it was a severe as was possible.[81]

Gyddyn came to me once the council had concluded. He sat on the ground beside me.

'The blood has come,' he said sadly.

'Yes.' I was in no mood for saying anything at length.

'It could not have been prevented. This act would doubtless have come to pass even if Miss Anna had not left Cythry.'

'I suppose.'

He stared straight ahead. We were facing Wigau and

---

[81] At this time the most severe punishment for theft would have been a lengthy prison sentence and a period of hard labour.

beyond it was Yr Elen and Llewellyn and Dafydd.

'You must return to Cythry, Faban-Morfa. Deliver the paintings into the hands of these evil men so that when the soldiers come we can be quickly rid of them. In the meantime I feel that Miss Anna will be safer if she comes with my people.'

'Where are you going?'

'It has been decided that the Frodorion farmers are to travel to Goddionduon. We shall be safe there." Goddionduon, or Llyn Goddionduon as it should more correctly be termed, lies within Gwydir. It is reserved as a place for feasting and celebration but also acts as a refuge for the farmers in times of hardship. They spent much of the Edwardian conquest of 1282 there, for example. It was far enough away and deep enough inside the forest that all the Frodorion would be safe there, as would Anna.

'When do you leave?'

'As soon as myself and Taicochion return. Eilio has ridden ahead to help the village prepare.'

'My guns are still there,' I remembered. Having left Dulyn in such a hurry I had not thought to bring them.

'Shall you need them, Faban-Morfa?' Gyddyn was

disapproving. 'I think not, Faban-Morfa. If you do, by any circumstance, need such foul weapons you have many more beneath your fortress... Or do you forget what I have seen?' He placed a hand on my shoulder. At first I was alarmed but then I was honoured. It is not often that one is touched by a Frodorion in such a way. 'But I know you will not use them for evil. You have the heart of a true Welshman and you are a good and wise chieftan.'

At those words he left me and returned to his own people so that he could shepherd them through those troubling times.

-CHAPTER XX-

I returned through Bethesda, hailing a passing cart when I reached the high street. I must have looked a sight, covered by ash and dirt from being up at High Rachub, but nobody looked at me in any aghast way. By now word had spread of the atrocity and the people who saw me looked instead with sorrow and sympathy. They said not a word nor asked how I felt for, I assume to a certain degree, it was etched upon my countenance.

The cart I hailed was owned by a farmer who lived outside of Bethesda but he was happy to take me further. He had heard the singing and some of what had occurred up in the mountains and he was keen to hear *how* it happened. He asked me if I knew but I lied and said that I did not. He knew I was lying. He then talked incessantly on another matter and although I allowed it I ignored the prattle for the most part. When I was required to speak, to answer a question or to respond to a statement, I spoke as little as I could get away with, often one or two word sentences and never saying anything of importance. I did not, to my shame, make an amiable or welcoming travel companion and when the farmer dropped me on the far side of Llyn Ogwen I think that he was glad to be rid of me.

I walked the rest of the way, slowly, shuffling, and with a tiredness. In usual circumstances I might have admired the grandiose scenery about me, reflecting upon how lucky I was to live in such a place, but on that day I did not care for any of it. The Glyders had lost their glory. The Carneddau had lost their majesty. They were uninteresting lumps perpetuating the background of my geography.

Even Cythry, as I arrived, was different. It was just another village to me, another Welsh mountain village of exactly the same kind as you can find anywhere throughout the land.

It was also quiet and where usually I might have seen Rhonda smoking a pipe by the door to his inn or Evans the cut going about his duties there was no one. I was reminded of the day father died and the weeks which had followed. There had been such a silence about the village then for he had been much loved and everyone grieved for him. They were grieving again now, though not for anyone any of them knew on a personal level.

I was little pleased to catch the castle at various moments as I walked through the village. It looked to be a folly, an over the top monstrosity thrown down the side of the mountain. Hollow, both in itself and its aura, and like the mountains it had lost all interest to me. Coming up the road towards it I couldn't help but think that it lacked something, that something was missing.

This consideration was only deepened as I walked through the door into the entrance hall. Like the village there was silence and the whole building thrummed with it, unnaturally, but it was not for grief at the tragedy. Even when I was alone it was never silent like this. There was always a creak or some kind of noise coming from somewhere. In the few days of my absence it had changed but I was at a great loss as to explain how.

It took me ten minutes of wandering from room to room to work out what it was. It was Anna. For the short time she had been here there had been bustle, activity, life! There had hardly been any moment where something had not been going on. From the moment she arrived she had been making her presence known, be it through trying on and criticising various clothes from the stores or looking for a room in which to sleep. Now that she was no longer there the castle yearned for her, yearned for the life which she brought. I longed for her too. I had only been back for a matter of minutes but I was already realizing that I needed her, that I needed the life she brought. I missed her.

On top of my feelings over High Rachub it was too much. I could not stand to be around the place, at least not without Anna by my side to make things bearable. I thus ran from the castle, or more accurately strolled at a hefty pace, and was halfway down the track before I collided with Beddgelert who was walking in the opposite direction. In my state I hardly recognized him.

'Max?'

'Oh… Beddgelert. I am sorry,' I mumbled when I came to my senses.

'You've been at High Rachub?'

'Yes… It was most dreadful.' Beddgelert put an arm of tenderness around me.

'Come my boy. We can talk of it back at the castle.'

'No,' I protested, pulling away. 'If we must talk anywhere I would prefer it to be the inn.'

Beddgelert took on an air of hurt and placed a hand to his mouth.

'Oh Max… You haven't heard!'

'Heard what?'

Beddgelert once more put his arm around me and started to lead me back up the track to the castle. This time I did not protest.

Once we were seated in the drawing room Beddgelert rang for a member of staff and Sophia attended.

'Sophia… Get Mr Morfasson a large brandy, please my dear.' Sophia obeyed as though Beddgelert were her employer.

'Where is Belvedere?' I asked as she hurried to the sideboard. As she began to pour my brandy I noticed that she had begun to tremble. She did not answer my question. Nor did Beddgelert until I had my brandy in hand.

'Max… I am sorry to be the one to tell you this. Belvedere and Rhonda were the two who went to the Illyrian to parlay with the revolutionaries. As soon as John Douglas returned from your meeting yesterday and put forward the idea Belvedere volunteered. Nobody else particularly wanted to deal with them so nobody argued. It was then suggested, by Evans the horse, that two people would present a better case than one. We all drew straws and it was Rhonda who came up short. The pair set out at once and they were seen in the

Max & Anna

Illyrian presenting their case to the revolutionaries by one of your men, secretly sent there by John Douglas, and they were reported to have left in disappointment. They have not been seen or heard from since. We have scoured the road between here and Bethesda but there has been no sign of them or their cart. We do not think it is the work of the revolutionaries as your man only reported them leaving the Illyrian very early this morning, after we knew that Rhonda and Belvedere had disappeared.'

'And I suppose that my man at the Illyrian has not been heard from again either?'

'No Max. He has not.' I closed my eyes and prayed that he had not suffered the fate I feared the most, the fate of High Rachub.

'Who is he?' I asked with trepidation and still with my eyes closed.

'Caerwynn Roberts.'

Caerwynn. He had been a good man, in his prime during the time of my father, and I approved that it had been he who had gone to watch the revolutionaries. Alas it was all too easy to think of the horrid fate that might have befallen him. It could have been that he followed the revolutionaries into the mountains and when they began their assault on High Rachub he could not have stood and allowed such an evil act to be performed. I knew him well and I knew his nature would not allow it. He would have intervened, or attempted to, and he would have been cut down like all the others who tried to fight. Now he might be lying with the Frodorion dead on Moel Faban, unrecognized and assumed one of them. This is by no means the certain truth but as no trace of him has been found in the years since I regret to say that it is a likely scenario.

I swallowed my brandy in one swig. I was saddened, maddened and cut deep.

'What happened up at High Rachub Max?' Beddgelert asked.

'You really do not wish to know,' I said with a bitter tone. 'It is too frightful a thing to contemplate. Because of it the Frodorion are now fleeing to Llyn Goddionduon, taking Miss Anna with them for her safety.'

'That is good to hear… But it does not solve the issue of the revolutionaries.'

A small smile touched my lips.

'Miss Anna had the solution. These soldiers searching for

the missing paintings... Anna suggested we ensure they find the paintings in the hands of the revolutionaries.'

Beddgelert's response was a despairing sigh, not for the plan itself but for the fact that I had just, in an indirect way, admitted to having the paintings in my possession. He disapproved. He always disapproved of such actions.

'Someone needs to take the paintings and plant them in the rooms of the revolutionaries at the Illyrian. John Douglas would be the ideal fellow.'

'John Douglas is in bed with a chill,' Beddgelert said. I had no sympathy. Such is what happens when you stand atop a mountain in the rain.

'Then somebody else... And whilst that is happening we must learn of what became of Rhonda and Belvedere. There are not many places where the Ogwen road diverts between here and Bethesda so they must be close by.' I called again for Sophia, she had silently made her exit after serving my brandy, and had her fetch a map of the Ogwen road.

'They would not go beyond Cythry without making a report, even if it were only for one moment,' I concluded. 'So that must mean that they are somewhere in between... The thing we should concentrate on is the cart. Why is there no sign of the cart?'

I should point out that although I was still feeling extreme melancholy and grief now that I had something with which I could sink my teeth into it was not dragging me into so much despair. I perused that map with a great thoroughness. It took my mind further from the grief, though only whilst the problem was before me.

There were a number of farms on the Ogwen road with short tracks leading up to them, as well as a short detour along Nant Ffrancon at the far end.

'Have you searched down Nant Ffrancon?' Beddgelert answered in the affirmative. That left the farms as the only place the cart could have been taken.

One farm caught Beddgelert's eye, Tal y Llyn Ogwen. A curious place on the edge of this side of the lake. It was a series of buildings, not insubstantial, which from the road were well hidden by a veil of trees. It was entirely possible to not know or even forget they were there. It was also uninhabited, not a fit place to live these days and so it would be perfect for hiding something such as a cart when you did not want it found.[82]

It had been uninhabited for the last fifteen years, ever since the previous owner, who was John Ogwen and a regular visitor to the inn at Cythry, had passed. The farm had been sold at auction, despite numerous individual attempts by myself, Beddgelert and the Baron Penrhyn to acquire the place for ourselves, to a man who went by the name of Morgan Hammond. Ever since this man had set no foot in the region nor visited his farm nor let it to a willing landsman. It had fallen to ruin and was now only frequented by walkers walking around the shores of Llyn Ogwen, where they picnicked in the shelter of its walls.

It seemed a possibility but it begged another question. Why on earth would Belvedere and Rhonda go there?

---

[82] Tal Y Llyn Ogwen still stands, much as it did at the time this was written. The sole difference today is that many of the trees have been removed and it is no longer uninhabited. There's a lot of private property signs about.

-CHAPTER XXI-

Beddgelert opted to take the paintings to the Illyrian and in the meantime myself and Evans the horse would investigate the farm. We took only a pair of six shooter pistols from the gun room. Mounting horses, myself on that temperamental horse which I held so dear, we rode to where that veil of trees obscured the farm and an overgrown dirt track diverted from the road and through those said same veil of trees towards it.

Before following the path I lowered myself to the ground and examined it. Had the cart been down this way it would have left evidence of its presence behind. So few people came down here that such a thing was inevitable. I was correct, of course. Amongst the overgrown weeds of the track the cart had left two long ruts where its weight had flattened the undergrowth and cut into the moist earth beneath. They curved away from the road, coming from the direction of Bethesda, and then ran away down the track and through the trees.

A deliberate turn off? It once again set my mind

wondering as to why Rhonda and Belvedere would want to come to such a place.

Evans and I advanced through the veil of trees, leaving our horses tied up by the road. Our pistols were in hand by the time we reached the other side and we could see the old, decrepit farm before us. The air about there stank something foul and amongst the foulness was a whiff of something burning, a fire. There were people here… Or there had been at some recent point. And there, off to one side in front of the trees, was the cart too. Its wheels had been crudely hacked off but Evans was still able to recognize it as the cart which had been taken to Bethesda the day before.

We moved forwards to investigate further but pulled back when a crack rang out from the largest of the buildings, a gunshot.

'Don't shoot. We only mean to find what has become of our friends,' I called out to the gunman. There was another crack of gunfire that splintered one of the trees above our head, this time from a different building. I caught a glimpse of a figure lurking near this building, ready to again shoot at us, and I shot back. I missed and my bullet embedded itself into the wall of the building. The figure took aim and I ducked behind a tree with barely enough time to see a bullet whizz by the spot where I had been standing. Evans caught sight of the first gunman and fired. The man slipped away and Evans missed.

'Tell us what has become of our friends and we shall leave you in peace.'

This time I received a reply.

'We have your friends… If they are not dead already they soon will be.' It was an English voice, a cruel one with a hint of the midlands to it.

'We know who you are, Max Morfasson,' another voice called. It was a Midlands voice but not so cruel. 'If you do not leave now your friends will not be the only people who die this day.'

A shot from Evans was the only dignified response. It was fired in the direction of the second voice. Another was returned in kind. I fired two shots in the same direction but both missed. Then the first man fired again and nearly got Evans in the leg. Had he not serendipitously shifted to the side at the very instant of the gunshot he would have lost its use. Then there was another shot from the second man and the wood of the veil shattered over our heads. Evans went wide with his retaliating shot and it zinged off a slate on one of the rooftops.

Our two opponents grew bolder, thinking that they had us. Both men fired at once and Evans and I were showered by yet more splinters. One of them, which was particularly large, struck Evans under the eye and lodged there, partially blinding him. He fired one more shot but I know not where it went.

'Morfas,' he called out. I wasted a shot to make our enemy to duck for cover whilst I ran to him. "I can't fight like this,' he groaned.

'Get yourself well behind the trees. I'll see if I can't finish these men off somehow.'

I took Evans's gun from him and prepared to launch a final and desperate assault upon the farm house. As you are reading this volume you will be aware that I did not die but it was a damn close thing. I saw the first man by his building and without moving I made my aim at the precise same moment in which he was aiming for myself. I was in the crosshairs of the second man too and he shot first, fortunately going wide and striking the tree beside me. The first man made to make his move but before he could pull the trigger I took my chance.

The gun fell from his hands and he crumpled against the wall of the building, dead in an instant.

That left only the second gunman whom I caught sight of around the corner, crouched on the ground and reloading his gun.

Now was my opportunity to end this. I marched from the veil, gun's prepared.

'It's over man,' I shouted. 'Drop the weapon and we can converse like gentlemen.' His reaction was to dodge around the corner of the building, towards me, firing as he did so. This was an amateurish thing to do. Firing whilst leaping around a corner gives you less time to aim and the movement of your body is going throw out what little accuracy you have left by an enormous degree.[83] This is what happened here. I heard his bullet cutting the trees behind me, showering splinters over no one. It also had the downside, for him, of leaving that foolish man exposed and it was too much of a simple and regrettable task to strike him dead.

---

[83] It *is* possible to become skilled at firing like this but it takes an awful lot of practice.

I ran to the main farmhouse building. In the ruins of what had once been the kitchen I found both of the men I was looking for and more. Rhonda was already dead, pale and ghostly and lying in a red pool.

Next to him was Belvedere, eyes closed but alive. His hand was pressed against his slowly moving chest and his fingers were coated by blood. There was a symbol daubed onto the wall above him, in blood. In his blood It was the mark of SHEMBLE; diamond overlaying a circle with spikes coming from it.[84] I should not need to inform you that its presence identified the two gunmen who lay outside.

I hurried to Belvedere and I held him in my arms. He attempted a smile.

'Mr Morfas…'

'No Belvedere. Don't speak,' I said, trying to hold back my anguish.

'I… must Mr… Morfas.'

'Save your strength Belvedere.'

'The rev…o…lutionaries… They did not… come here…

---

[84] The mark of SHEMBLE is described somewhat differently throughout the annals of the Morfas family. Though always the same rough shape, it is sometimes referred to as a spider and sometimes as a spiky diamond. It is even, at one stage, described as a vagina.

alone. Two.... Two... SHEMBLE...'

'I know. I have dealt with them. They are dead.'

'They came as... as... guides for... the rev...o...lutionaries.'

'They kept apart from them? So that we would not notice they were with them?' Belvedere gave a weak nod. 'And when you tried to reason with the revolutionaries they stalked ahead to waylay you on your return?'

'Yes. But there is... more. They knew... knew that...'

'Knew what Belvedere?'

'They knew... Miss Anna... Not in Cythry.' I was puzzled. How could they know such a thing?

'How did they know Belvedere?'

There was no response. His soul had departed this cruel and most dreadful world.

I laid down my friend with gentility and as much tenderness, care and loyalty as he had shown to my family over his many years of service, before leaving the farmhouse.

It had already been an awful day and the two more needless deaths of Rhonda and Belvedere left me more cold, more numb and all the more melancholy. They were pointless, needless deaths.

Why had they died? Why had it been necessary to kill them? Was it because they were *my* men and these SHEMBLE agents were trying to send me a message, trying to prove how strong they were? Or was it for the reason that Rhonda and Belvedere had tried to interfere with the revolutionaries?

Whatever the reason, killing them had been a cold, heartless and wicked thing to do.

-CHAPTER XXII-

I came back to the road to find that Evans had removed the splinter from beneath his eye. It had left a thwacking great and bloody gash across his face.

'We must get you back to Cythry and see to that wound,' I said in an aloof and curt manner.

'What of Rhonda and Belvedere?' From the way in which he winced I guessed that it was painful for him to speak. I was too numb to answer him and mounted my horse instead.

We would make progress slowly for the sake of Evans but we had not gone more than a few metres before we were stopped by the sight of twelve red coated soldiers, all mounted, coming up the road in our direction. These could only be the ones who came for the paintings and whilst there was a need to return Evans to Cythry it would do no harm to stop and point these gentlemen in the direction of the Illyrian.

'Good god man… What happened to you?' the captain asked as he came to a halt before us. He then noticed Evans and the gash across his face.

'It is a long story but I believe it involves the same men whom you seek.'

'We seek those who stole a group of valuable paintings from the Baron Penrhyn.'

'Then it does indeed involve the same men. They are Romanian revolutionaries seeking vengeance upon a princess who has been at my house this last week. They have committed several evil acts in attempting to learn her location and I have come to learn that *they* stole the paintings so that they may sell them and return payment to the men who backed their revolution.' The captain looked upon with me interest.

'You are, by chance, Max Morfasson?'

'I am indeed.' I smiled at him in the hope that it would assist my case.

'Good,' the captain responded. 'The baron informed me that you could be trusted in helping to retrieve the paintings if necessary.'

Now ***there*** was a surprise. The baron trusting *me*? Such a thing had never before happened in the entire history of creation.

'Where are these men now?'

'They are in Bethesda, at the head of the valley, though they have this morning been at large in the mountains. I can lead you to where they stay if only someone will escort my man home so that he may tend his wound.'

It was done. One of the soldiers was assigned to escort Evans whilst myself and the remainder of the brigade rode for Bethesda, myself and the captain leading the charge.

As we rode I explained how prince Gustaff had assigned me to Anna's protection and how we had been followed back here to Ogwen. The captain was most interested to learn that she was currently under the care of the Frodorion. He was a scholar of their ways, I discovered, and longed to make their acquaintance but knew such a thing was impossible owing to his profession.

I revealed the deed performed at High Rachub and of how two of the men, I saw no need to mention that they were SHEMBLE, had taken Belvedere and Rhonda to Tal Y Llyn Ogwen. To prevent him sending soldiers back to the farm to investigate I assured him that all business up there had been concluded and seen to by my own people.

The captain did not mention it but I could see that he was impressed by his surroundings. For several reasons I did not see all he saw in quite the same way, one of which was my melancholy and numbness. I can guess that the mountains soared higher than any had soared before them and that Llyn Ogwen glittered more golden than any other lake under an afternoon sun. Such is always the way with first time visitors. They are always impressed by what they see.

'You are lucky to live in such a place,' he remarked as we rode the high road above Nant Ffrancon. 'When my commission expires I should like to retire here, perhaps buy some land and become a farmer.'

'Land does not often come up for sale in these parts I am sorry to say. Perhaps if you asked him very nicely the baron will reward you with one of his tenancies as a reward for the recovery of his paintings.' The captain made an appreciable gesture.

'That is a wonderful suggestion. I shall bring the matter to him when I make my report.'

'Whilst we are talking of the baron,' I diverted, 'why did he call on men from Chester when there is a garrison at Caernarfon?'

'He was owed a favour by our commander in chief, the Duke of Westminster. It must have been easier for him to involve *us* than it was to involve these other fellows or the local police force.'

Ah… So nothing to do with mistrust or suspicion or slighting the local inhabitants, it was all the returning of a favour. It was nothing personal and from the way the captain claimed that I was to be trusted it was also clear that the baron had few suspicions regarding my involvement. Perhaps he considered that in as much as we disagreed I would not debase myself to such low, vindictive and criminal behaviour as stealing his paintings.

We came to the end of Nant Ffrancon and were soon riding the final stretch of Dyffryn Ogwen into Bethesda. Here the road curves and bucks around the last remnants of the Glyders and around the edge of the slate quarry before diving into the heart of Bethesda's jaw.

The end of the working day was approaching and so as we entered the town we passed by the slate workers, dusty and weary and in need of sustenance. They looked upon us agog, thundering by on our horses, and myself in particular. I was set apart by my dust and my nightshirt which all looked far shabbier than they were when compared to the neatly pressed and clean cut red coats of the soldiers.

The Illyrian was a hovel of a place and it could not have been less welcoming in its appearance. The lime render had once been white but now, where it had not flaked away to reveal cheap brick work, it was a grubby sort of grey. Slates were missing from the roof, remnants of them littering the bottom edge of the building and the gutter. The windows on the first floor were each cracked and all of them, that is to say the windows across the entire building, were so grimy and blackened that it was impossible to see through them. This meant that natural light could not penetrate inside and it was always gloomy and full of shadows that flickered in the gaslight.

Leaving our horses tied to a horse post, they still had them outside such places in those days, we entered into this den of iniquity. The red uniforms of the soldiers provided a stark contrast to the dusty and glum décor. There were few clientele about, only an old man in the corner who looked as though he had been there since opening time. There was also Beddgelert but his soul would never forgive me if I referred to him as a client of the Illyrian. He was seated at the bar with a tumbler half full of brandy. There was no sign of the revolutionaries.

The hulking great brute of a doorman, a leech who called himself Augustus Malvolio, approached us.

'Sirs,' he spoke in a deep and pompous voice. 'How may I assist you all this day?' His eyes wandered in my direction and he looked at my state with contempt.

'We seek men,' the captain declared. Before he could clarify himself Malvolio grasped the wrong part of the stick.

'Alas sir, we do not have anyone employed in that way at present but if you are willing to wait there are always other miscreants of that persuasion in here of an evening.' He was disgusted by the idea, I could see it written all over his face, but he was such a sycophant that he would do anything to please anyone who looked like they had the remotest slither of power.

'You misunderstand. The men we seek are criminals, wanted for the theft of valuable paintings belonging to the Penrhyn estate. They are foreign gentlemen who speak little English.'

'We have several of that type sir. There is a gentleman who keeps to himself and there are several less kempt persons who share a single room.'

'It is probably the latter whom we seek though it will do no harm to interrogate the former either. If you could show them down to us...'

'The former is here sir but the latter all went out in the early hours and have yet to return.'

'Then if we may search their rooms?'

'Certainly sir...'

Malvolio guided the soldiers away upstairs whilst I made for Beddgelert and the bar.

'The ephemera are in their place?' I asked with a raised eyebrow.

'They are indeed. What have you found of Rhonda and Belvedere?'

'Dead. The revolutionaries were accompanied by SHEMBLE guides. Staying elsewhere I assume. On their return from attempting to reason with the revolutionaries these SHEMBLE guides waylaid Belvedere and Rhonda and killed them both.'

Beddgelert put a hand on my shoulder.

'Oh Max. I am sorry. Is there anything which I may do for you?'

'Order me a stiff drink,' I sniffed rudely. Beddgelert only smiled in a caring way.

'Of course. Mr Hodge?' he called to the barman. 'Your stiffest drink if you don't mind.'

It was a double vodka, a drink I do not usually care for but swallowed all the same.[85] It left a burning feeling in my throat which I was grateful for.

'This is for you Belvedere,' I announced after ordering a second. 'May you serve the lord with as much loyalty as you served my family.'

'And for Rhonda,' Beddgelert added. 'And Codswallop and all the people of High Rachub.'

'Yes. To all who have fallen foul of these wicked men.' We both shot our drinks.

It was two minutes and a lifetime later that two of the soldiers returned carrying a small man under one shoulder each. He did not scream or struggle but he looked alarmed. The only movement he made was to prevent the ovoid spectacles which rested on his nose from falling away. He was far too respectable looking to be frequenting a place like the Illyrian and I thought that he could not have chosen to stay here through any prior knowledge of the place.

---

[85] Max is lying. Just like my dearest (I don't mean that) brother Will he drank it like tap water.

He was deposited on a table and the soldiers stood before him, blocking the view from the bar with their arms folded.

'What do you know of the other men staying here?' one of the soldiers demanded.

'I know that they are wicked men,' the little man answered in a confidant but high pitched voice. 'They are revolutionaries from Ardeluta... Romania... They usurped the royal family and now they hunt for them in revenge.' The soldiers and I had the same thought in response.

'How do you know this? Have you spoken to them? Are you one of them?'

'No I am almost certainly *not* one of them. I have not spoken to them either. I have done my best to avoid them from the moment I heard them arrive.'

'You knew as soon as you heard them that they were revolutionaries?' The soldier asking the question did so with a great suspicion.

'Of course I knew that they were revolutionaries.'

'How?' There was no response. I could not see the man but I could imagine him shuffling and twitching nervously on his table. 'How?' the same soldier again demanded. 'How did you know they were revolutionaries?'

There was still no answer.

'It's curious,' Hodge the barman whispered to myself and Beddgelert. 'I've not heard him speak English this well before now. It's always been broken, poor. There have even been times when he hasn't understood things at all.'

'As if he has only been *pretending* that he can't speak English?'

'Precisely that!'

'How long has he been here?' I was beginning to suspect that this man might be someone of great importance.

'About a month by my reckoning. He rarely leaves his room and I don't think I've seen him since the other men first came a few days back.'

'Most curious indeed.' Beddgelert was coming to the same conclusions as myself. 'Max… Do you suppose that you have had prior dealings with this gentleman?'

'Beddgelert, I think I may well have done.' It was the first time I had smiled since leaving Dulyn.

Before I could intervene and approach the captain came striding into the bar with a rolled up painting in his hand. He appeared angry.

'What do you know of this?' He pushed his subordinates

aside and thrust the painting at the man. The man, who I could now see more clearly and who was starting to resemble an image locked at the back of my mind, took the painting and unrolled it. When he saw what lay upon the canvas his face glowed and he beamed from ear to ear.

'This is a Rembrandt. I would know one anywhere. I did not expect that I would ever see one in a place like this.'

'It was stolen some days ago from a nearby estate.'

'By those accursed revolutionaries I presume?'

'Yes. By those accursed revolutionaries as you called them.'

'That's what they think,' Hodge grinned quietly. Hodge was a good man and you could always rely on him to be discrete with any underhand deeds.

'Where are these revolutionaries now?' the captain sneered, snatching back the painting.

'How am I supposed to know? I am not one of them. I have been avoiding them.'

'Why? And how did you know that they were revolutionaries?' one of the subordinate soldiers cut in, slamming his fist down on the table and causing the little man to bounce. He did not answer, nonetheless.

'Answer him… How did you know?' the captain barked when he grew tired of the silence.

'I think that I can tell you that,' I said from the bar. The little man at first gave me a frightened look and then one of disgust. 'The revolutionaries must return here at some stage… Their possessions are here, yes?' Hodge and the soldiers all nodded. 'Then all shall be made clear when they return.'

'Who are you sir? How does a vagabond like yourself know of my affairs?' The man looked aggrieved.

'All in good time. I would like to enquire of yourself a little first. How is it that a man such as you finds himself in this den?'

'That is none of your concern. I will admit that it is not my usual sort of residence but my current circumstances have necessitated it.' He folded his arms and lifted his nose to the ceiling. Priggish.

He lowered it again when the remaining soldiers entered, carrying with them all of the paintings. He looked shocked and appalled and as one soldier passed he took a painting from him and unrolled it.

'Good lord… How were these rogues able to steal such

Max & Anna

wonderful paintings?'

'There was a lady... She called herself Lady Botterly and pretended that she was a friend of the baron to whom these paintings belong. She was able to take them by convincing the staff that she was acting on the orders of the baron. She has since fled the area,' I explained. The man looked me up and down as though I were dirt.

'Then why did this lady not take the paintings when she fled? Why are they still here with the revolutionaries?'

'That we do not yet know,' I replied with haste, fearing that whatever other answer I gave would bring the whole plan down around our ears. 'But hopefully we shall discover the reason when the revolutionaries are locked up in Caernarfon Gaol.'

'And how will you find this woman if she has already fled?'

'I have a man on her trail as we speak. If he is not able to find her then I fear that no one ever shall.'

'A man?'

He again searched me with his eyes and then his face shone in horror as he came to the realization of who I was. He plunged down from the table and walked slowly towards me. He peered up at my face and then pushed his spectacles up into the bridge of his nose with a single finger.

'For a man of your reputation, Mr Morfasson, I expected a more civilized individual.'

I blushed.

'It has been a long day, sir. I do not usually roam the world in such an ugly state I assure you,' I excused.

'Max is one of the most civilized people I know,' Beddgelert praised. 'He has more class than all of the English aristocracy combined.' I further reddened at the compliment.

'And who are you sir?' The man did not sound impressed.

'The Earl of Beddgelert. I am assisting Max with his endeavours.' On hearing that Beddgelert was an earl the man gave a pleased and excitable bow before turning back to me.

'And what of my daughter sir? I assigned her to your protection, if you recall. Where is she?'

'She is safe. Once the revolutionaries have been brought to justice then I shall be happy to take you to her.'

Speaking of the revolutionaries it was now that they entered the stage. They were a sorry looking bunch; unkempt, unshaven and dressed in ragged, dirty clothes, looking as though they had all the cares of the world upon their shoulders.

They rattled into the building and then stopped when they noticed that the bar was full of soldiers. Their presence worried them but this worry turned into an incredible and unexpected shock when the little man stepped forwards to greet them with a smug grin upon his face. He knew that at last he was safe from them so there was no longera need to hide himself.

'Gentlemen,' Prince Gustaff said, bursting with laughter.

-CHAPTER XXIII-

The revolutionaries were still in a state of shock when the soldiers took them away to Caernarfon Gaol. Then there was a large degree of explaining to be done both on my own part and on the part of Prince Gustaff. We left Beddgelert at the Illyrian, I rode my own horse and Prince Gustaff borrowed Beddgerlert's, and we made our explanations as we rode towards Cythry. Prince Gustaff took the first turn.

It was a ploy on his part. He knew of the Illyrian by reputation and he considered that it was the last place in all the world where the revolutionaries would expect to find him. He was quite right on that front. It was the last place in the world where *anyone* would expect to find him.[86] As we know, the extraordinarily slim chance of those revolutionaries turning up in the exact same place had come to pass and Prince Gustaff was angrily determined to discover the reason why this had happened.

---

[86] A scribble in the back of the original manuscript, in the handwriting of my Great Uncle Seamus, claims that other members of the Aredelutian royal family were hiding in equally disreputable taverns elsewhere in Europe. This is not true.

I concocted a tale of how SHEMBLE must have identified my men in Paris and how they had helped the revolutionaries to follow myself and Anna here to the mountains. It was a story I would become used to telling over the following years, for reasons that will soon become clear.

Prince Gustaff was scathing in his response to it. He reprimanded me, saying that I should have been more careful and alert, especially in so far as his daughter's safety was concerned.

He was more pleased with what I told him of our (myself and Anna's) exploits, pleased that I had given her so much enjoyment during her time with me. He laughed as though I were pulling his leg when I told him how she had ingratiated herself with the villagers of Cythry.

'You are having a jest Mr Morfasson,' he ticked. 'I know my daughter and she is not one to mingle in such a free fashion with the likes of your villagers. She would pull her nose in disgust at such an idea.'

'It is quite true I assure you, sir. She is quite taken with the Welsh people, especially my village. As of this moment she is with a good friend of mine. He is a hill farmer.' Prince

Gustaff wobbled with laughter.

'This I must see with my own eyes!'

We came briefly to Cythry where we left our horses with Mrs Evans. Whilst I washed, shaved and redressed, Prince Gustaff insisted that Sophia and Constance take him upon a guided tour of the castle. He was like a young child on Christmas morning, full of squeals and exclamations. He asked lots of questions, pointing to every painting and wanting to know who they were of and who they were by and what the people in the paintings did in their lives. He was so inquisitive that by the time I had finished my refreshment his tour was only half way up the staircase between the ground and first floors. He was sad to be dragged off but he at least accepted that the reasoning behind it was a sound one.

Now with a cart and fresh horses, overhung by an oil lantern, we set out for Goddionduon.

We rode out past Capel Curig and then at Pont Cyfyng we turned off the road and into the forest of Gwydir, following an increasingly less worn dirt track where gnarled and oppressive trees reached out to swipe and scratch at us. The horses hated it, they were afraid, but like faithful troops they carried on into the trees, into where the only light was our lantern and all about was shadows and danger.

It was foolish coming in here alone as we might easily have lost ourselves forever. We went slowly and I made a mental map of our road as we travelled along. After an hour both Prince Gustaff and I were beginning to regret setting off on this journey, he thought that we were lost. Then ahead of us we saw a small light. I allowed it to grow larger and brighter and then stopped the cart.

'If you wouldn't mind waiting here sir, just for a moment. I will see if it is safe for us to approach.'

'How do you mean safe? These people would not harm *me* would they?'

'They might if they thought you meant *them* harm.' Prince Gustaff snorted back at me in the same way Anna did when she was disgusted by something.

We had, or more accurately our lantern had, already been sighted by the Frodorion watchers and as I approached I heard 'Halt! Who are you? Y Lembo Gwyrion?' in Welsh.

'I am no Y Lembo Gwyrion. I am Faban-Morfa of Cythry, accompanied by the crown Prince Gustaff of Ardeluta, father of Miss Anna.' There was a long, tense pause in the darkness and I imagined a whispered discussion taking place between the watchers.

Eilio stumbled from the trees, spear in hand and a smile upon his face. We bowed to each other.

'Faban-Morfa. I am pleased to see you. You have dealt with the evil men?'

'I have,' I returned. 'They rot in Caernarfon Gaol. I have much else to tell for I regret that more blood has been spilled this day.'

'That tale must wait Faban-Morfa. There is more pressing news awaiting you in the encampment.' He started to walk towards the light and I hesitated, wondering about Prince Gustaff. Eilio called back to reassure me.

'Never fear Faban-Morfa. The other watchers will take care of him.' Despite his reassurance I was still worried. It was not beneath the Frodorion to leave him out here, to not allow him into the encampment. But I carried on inside regardless and forgot these fears. I was eager to see Anna.

It was a wooded glade, resting a few trees back from the shores of the lake. It had all the appearance of a carnival but none of the atmosphere. Around a blazing bonfire in the centre of the encampment were around three circles of brightly coloured and garish tents. They were small and narrow things but still high enough for an average sized man to comfortably stand up in. They numbered I do not know how many because I could not count the ones on the rear rows but there were enough for all the Frodorion farmers of the Carneddau. Above the door of each one hung a coloured lantern, though they were all unlit. Of the people, they all either sheltered in their tents or stood in the doorways, looking aloof and worried and mournful, staring towards the fire with melancholy, without hope and without joy.

Anna approached as I entered and she was as melancholy looking as the Frodorion.

'Mr Max,' she began crisply. Her tone suggested she had been offended by something and she was about to bring me to task for it. That was not the case. 'This may shock you and I am not pleased by it, but I should tell you that we are to be married.'

'I beg your pardon?' was all I was able to say in response.

'We are to be married,' Anna repeated curtly.

'Miss Anna… What in God's name has put this silly notion into your head?'

'The women of the Frodorion say that my dreams foretell

it and it is inevitable.'

'Have you spoken of your dreams again?'

'Nothing of the sort…' Maeneira came up behind me and frightened the life from my body. 'She has the abyss within her and none would dare attempt such a thing. We have merely discussed what was seen before. We have talked of the abyss and have concluded that it can mean but one thing… She is Morfa.' I choked on air, more shocked than I was when Anna declared we were to be married.

'She can't be. The abyss within her must have some other meaning,' I protested. I was tempted to flat out deny the claims of the Frodorion, claim that dream interpretation was hokum but cowardice and a lifetime of respect for these folks stayed my hand.

'We have searched for other possible meanings but there are none. As I recall your father, Marw Morfa[87] Albert was loyal to his wife, never straying?'

'Most certainly.'

'So there is no chance that she was born Morfa. That can

---

[87] After a Morfasson dies, in Frodorion custom, they are referred to as 'Marw Morfa.' In English it translates to Dead Marsh. In order to distinguish who is being spoken of their first name is usually added.

only mean one thing. She will one day carry Morfa within her womb… Your child, Faban Morfa.' I almost fainted and again wanted to debunk it as nonsense. There was no way they could tell, just from a dream reading, that Anna would one day carry my child. 'If you have any honour you shall marry her.'

'I… I refuse to believe it,' I stammered.

I walked away, rude of me I know, and went to find Gyddyn. Perhaps *he* would agree that this was nonsense.

He was resting alone in his tent at the far side of the encampment, close to where I could hear the waters of Llyn Goddionduon lapping against its shores.

'You have heard?' he asked as I entered.

'Yes but I do not believe it,' I said truthfully. Gyddyn nodded in understanding.

'Neither did Miss Anna when Maeneira first told her of the women's conclusion. She made an enormous scene, mostly in her native tongue.'

'So what changed her mind?'

'She looked into her heart. After I calmed her down I told her to forget the child and to reflect on what she *really* thought of you, regardless if the prophecy of jer dreams come to pass or no. I suggest you do the same. *Can* you see yourself spending the remainder of your days with that woman?' He stood and left me to contemplate the answer.

After twenty minutes of thought I came to conclusion that I *could* see myself with her for the rest of my days. The answer was a most definite yes. I could no longer see life without her. Without her Cythry and the village were empty and the thoughts of romancing other women, of marrying any woman other than Anna, seemed appalling. It came like a bolt from the blue but I realized that I was head over heels in love with that infuriating Romanian princess.

As the revelation hit me something in my brain clicked and I decided that I really *did* want to marry her as soon as possible. I previously believed such overly sentimental thoughts the product of ridiculous Penny Dreadfuls but here I was living them for real.

Prince Gustaff had by now been allowed entry into the encampment. Eilio and another had spent ten minutes instructing him in etiquette before allowing it, however. He was conversing with Anna upon the far side of the bonfire. It was not a happy conversation though I could not understand a word. Prince Gustaff was protesting something and Anna sounded as though she were attempting to change his mind. I ignored the fact that they were talking and marched right over in order to interrupt. This matter could not wait.

'Prince Gustaff,' I began firmly. 'Concerning my payment for protecting your daughter. There is but only one thing which I would gladly accept- Her hand in marriage.'

Anna was frozen by my statement. I would have said she was appalled by the idea if she had not been the one who first put it to me. Meanwhile, Prince Gustaff had turned a funny colour.

'I cannot accept that Mr Morfasson,' he said calmly. 'Anna has already requested my permission and I have denied her also. You shall not marry whilst there is breath in my body.'

'Then we shall live in sin, father,' Anna intruded determinedly. I could have run from the encampment at the prospect. I was not completely dead against that idea but the scandal of it would ruin both myself and my business. 'I will admit I am not entirely thrilled by the prospect of marrying him but if I must then I must, regardless of what you say.'

Prince Gustaff gave a sigh of resignation. He knew better than I have ever done that arguing with Anna once she has set her mind on something is a Sisyphean task.

'Are you sure this what you wish my dear? This man may well be a fine gentleman, or he has a fine home at the least, but he is not a suitable husband for a princess.' Anna took my hand.

'But I am not a princess. I have not been a princess since those blasted revolutionaries drove us from Romania.' Prince Gustaff, who in contrast would always consider himself to be Crown Prince of Ardeluta until his dying day, surrendered completely with a heavy sigh.

'Well… If that is your wish my dear then I shall not stand in your way.'

Things moved faster than I would have liked.

No less than an hour later Anna and I were married. Gyddyn performed a traditional Frodorion ceremony with lots of singing and merriment.

Then, for one night, which did not seem long enough, all that had previously happened, all the pains and the heartaches and the grief, were forgotten in the joys of our union. They would return by morning and the mourning would last for many months. Some of the Frodorion would never recover. They would die mourning their fallen brethren.

Max & Anna

But for one moment there was joy

-CHAPTER XXIV-

Here I reach the end of my tale and there only remains to tell of what has occurred during the near thirty years of my marriage.

For the theft of the paintings the revolutionaries were each sentenced to twenty years hard labour and not one of them lived to see the end of their sentence. They died in the toils of their punishment and I do not think they ever knew that it was the object of their heinous endeavours who was the real culprit behind their crime.

The English soldiers, following the successful completion of their task, spent a week in the Illyrian where it has been reported that a number of them caught that awful venereal disease, *Vaginum-rhamno*. What happened to them afterwards I do not know, except for the captain. The baron granted his request for land and gave him a smallholding on the far side of Bangor. He married a local girl and since his death four years back that small holding has been tended by his eldest son. He had three children, two sons and a daughter, and his second son is serving in the same regiment as his father before him.

Of the others mentioned in this tome only myself, Anna and Eilio still live. Prince Gustaff had only seen the end of the century by a few weeks when a stroke took him in the dead of night. He had lived out his days with his wife and son (who has never married) in a Venetian palazzo, dreaming of regaining his kingdom. He never fully accepted me as his son-in-law but he tolerated me, knowing that Anna and I loved each other and nothing in the world could change that.

John Douglas, dear John Douglas whom I shall never forget, worked until the last breath left his body in the year eighteen eighty four. We found him stone cold at his desk, staring out of the window with a smile upon his face. His last wish was to be buried in his native Jamaica and I considered it no bother to go to the expense of making it happen. He would be an impossibly old man if he yet lived but when dealing with his inferior successors I have often wished such a thing were so.

Evans the horse followed him a year after and Beddgelert, who was a silly sod and tumbled over the edge of a precipice whilst out walking in the mountains, followed another year after that. He, Beddgelert, was succeeded by his then young son but we are not on the friendliest of terms. Beddgelert's Will stated that I was to act as mentor to the boy but he has never once heeded my advice and has often taken the opposite course of action. In my personal opinion he is a considerable ass.

Even the Baron Penrhyn lies in his grave, as does his successor. The last and the current barons I have found to be more decent, amicable chaps than the first and they have a greater love for the land and the people than their predecessor.

At times I have even admired them but their decency has not stopped Anna from making it her continuing mission to be a thorn in their side. Over the years she has done all she can think of to annoy, irritate and cajole them. What she hopes to achieve is beyond me for I have never asked and have merely allowed her to go about her business. Recently the quarrymen of Bethesda struck for better pay, a walkout that lasted three exhausting years, and it will not surprise you to learn that Anna played a key role in organising it.

Eilio now leads the Dulyn Frodorion and has done so ever since the harsh winter of eighty one took the lives of many

Frodorion across the mountains. The dead included Maeneira, Gyddyn, Taicochion and Ywda. I worry for the future of the Frodorion farmers. They have never before been ones to mix outside their own community but since the turn of the century the youth have been carelessly abandoning their roots and culture in favour of what I can only call a more common way of life. Many have left the mountain pastures and are working and living in places like Bangor and Caernarfon and Caergybi. I even met one in Paris last year, would you believe. Even amongst those young who have stayed in the mountains it is not unusual to see them roaming the streets of Bethesda, drinking in the taverns and whoring in the dens. If things continue in this manner then I fear the farmer's lifestyle will die out altogether.[88]

Anna and I took a while to get used to the idea of marriage. Having been through no proper courtship things were awkward and strange between us and after a week both of us started to think that Gyddyn and Maeneira had

---

[88] Whilst it is still possible to find some half-Frodorion today, Frodorion culture is extinct and they have been almost entirely forgotten as a group.

unscrupulously tricked us into marriage. Indeed, they did, but as the months and years have gone by we have come to understand what they always knew. We were in love with each other from the moment Anna stepped onto that foul smelling dockyard in London. Their trickery was only the push we needed to admit our love, both to ourselves and each other.

She is the same as she ever was. She is still priggish, opinionated and determined to have her own way but I would not have her changed. I am an old man now and I can feel my years as the head of the family weighing on my shoulders. Anna pulls me through, helping where she can, and I know it shall not be long before I can leave it behind and pass it all to the next generation.

For several years Anna and I thought that there might not be a next generation. It took us a full year to begin to talk seriously of children but we were not blessed until Anna gave birth to a boy some seven years ago. He, we named him Montgomery but call him Monty, is much like his mother. He is opinionated, has an air of the high class about him, and pouts in the same manner when he does not get his own way. However, he knows that he *can't* always have things his own way. Unlike his mother he *will* concede defeat but he will always sulk for some time afterwards.

Anna and I, because it has always been so, still refer to each other as Mr Max and Miss Anna and when he was young Monty would walk around insisting on being called Mr Monty. He has had to settle for being Master Monty until he is older and although he agreed he walked around with a pout for a full two weeks. I am proud to say that he has a good head on his shoulders and he will one day make a fine leader of men.

Much else is the same. The mountains are still here, unchanging, as is Cythry and the village. Bethesda, now minus the Illyrian, is still a mining town. The quarry is still the biggest employer and the town still has its seedy underbelly. I hope it always shall for it gives the place life. Bangor is a sorrier city without its opera house but quite soon it shall rise from its ashes. A new architectural gem is soon to grace its skyline, a university building on the hill overlooking the city, shaped like a grand citadel.

I think back to those days when I first met Anna and I reflect upon the great losses we all endured, the Frodorion in particular. Anna, indirectly, brought pain and misery and heartache in her wake. She really *did* bring blood to the land. But I would go through it all again just for the sake of being with that wonderful woman.

APPENDIX

-CHAPTER 7-

The following was included in the original manuscript as chapter seven but myself and James have removed it to here because we thought it a bit long and superfluous to the rest of the story. It bogged the flow down, if you understand what I mean- Marco

Over the following three days I forgot about the warning of the Frodorion and spent much of them in a carefree manner, showing Anna about my homeland, Morfasson country as some guides prefer to call it. The definition of Morfasson country is a broad one but I personally consider that it begins at Afon Conwy in the east and runs down to Betws-Y-Coed in the south where the boundary then traverses the edge of Moel Siabod and follows the road up to and through Bwlch Llanberis, continuing until it reaches Caernarfon where it meets the sea at the southern end of the Sain Cerddoriaeth, before following the coast back to Afon Conwy. It is, therefore, a sizeable land which includes a good deal of beauty and wonder.

To the north is the sea, specifically Bae Conwy, and its shores are lined by shingled beaches in the east and the mud flats of Traeth Lafan in the west. Before Telford built his famous bridge across the Cerddoriaeth men and women would walk across these tidal flats to catch a boat over to Beaumaris and Mon. Many lost their lives in the attempt and their bodies and possessions were washed out into the Irish Sea or swallowed by the flats, never to be seen again. None but the foolish set foot on these treacherous flats now, thanks entirely to that marvellous wonder that is Mr Telford's bridge, and I dearly hope that there should never again come a time when men should walk Traeth Lafan.

The eastern beaches, in summer, are frequented by day trippers and holiday makers, those who wish to avoid the crowds and popular bustle of Llandudno across the far side of the Conwy. The shingle means that the children cannot build the spectacular castles of sand which they might on other beaches but it does not stop them trying. Some will pile the shingle into large mounds so that their castles look more like cairns or fallen pyramids whilst the cleverer ones take a different approach and lay the shingles flat like dry stone walls so that what results is a unique and impressive little building. They last longer than their sandy counterparts (if built in a strong fashion) able to last for several tides before inevitably being knocked back to the ground from whence they came.

The shingle beaches come to an abrupt end at the Afon Conwy a glorious river. It enters the sea through a narrow strip with Deganwy upon the far bank and Y Bannau on our own side. There is a lighthouse here, not a grand or a spectacular lighthouse, it is more a beacon now that I think about it, but a lighthouse nonetheless. The river widens out at the town of Conwy and here the waters deposit their sediment so that the river runs in strands between high bars and banks where it is often the case that you can espy fisher boats berthed on them. At high tide it is a wonderful place. The waters run deep and tranquil whilst the narrow entrance to the sea and two high grounded shores on either side make it appear safe and protected, an ideal harbour.

Further on the river again narrows and it becomes a winding, picturesque lady of beauty. The high shores drop away and what is left is a wide and fertile plain on either side. It is wider on the western edge but on both shores this plain eventually rises again, to rolling hills in the east and stately peaks in the west. Tributaries flow off at various points, up towards the mountains and north of Dolgarrog in particular, before the river becomes so narrow that it is no more than a stream, several delicious islands have formed.

And then, as I say, the river becomes so narrow that it is no more than a stream. But what a stream it is, dear reader. It cascades and bubbles and dances over many rocks and obstacles, all the while now surrounded by the expansive forest of Gwydir, a place that is ancient and foreboding and has given rise to all kinds of lore concerning elves and fearies and nymphs. It is a place of magic, they say, and any man who goes into those woods alone is a brave man indeed.

At the heart of the forest lies Betws-Y-Coed and the south eastern corner of Morfasson country. It is a sleepy place where little of significance ever occurs but the local folk will be happy to greet you and they are pleasant enough to guide you about the forest for a small fee.

Many of the outsiders who come here are artists and romantics. Turner, the famous Turner, came here once upon a time. Artists are always welcome and it is no surprise that they do come when you see how beautiful it is. Words cannot describe what must be seen with one's own eyes in order to fully appreciate. Betws is a patch of paradise, a shan-gri-la.

Going west along the southern boundary you begin to follow the course of Afon Llugwy, not a great river, as far as Capel Curig. Much of what lies to either side is still the forest of Gwydir but to the south, as you approach Capel Curig, the rocky tor of Moel Siabod comes into view. The sight but pails into comparison with what is to come further along the southern boundary of the region.

Past Capel Curig the road continues along the length of Moel Siabod but it is vastly overshadowed by your first sight of the Glyderau to the north. They will stay with you a while as their southern flanks are themselves a part of the boundary of Morfasson country. From here they look wild and imposing. Grassy lowlands rise up into black, vertical cliffs scarred by crevices and boulders and scree slopes and the further you follow the southern boundary the closer you find yourself to them. By the time you reach Bwlch Llanberis you are right up against them. They tower over you so high that it feels as though they might fall down upon you.

And to the south, almost touching those Glyder, is Yr Wyddfa and it is no less terrifying. Its northern slopes rise up in the same vertical fashion and you begin to wonder how on earth any man has ever conquered this ancient volcano. But then, too quickly, it is behind you and you reach the twin lakes of Padarn and Peris. They are lovely lakes in their own right but they are, alas, forever stained by the blemish of the Dinorwig quarry cutting into the mountain above them. You are better off standing with your back to that abomination, looking across the lakes to where the foothills of Yr Wyddfa appear more gentle and pleasing. There is even a castle here, a little round one by the name of Dolbadarn. A short walk beyond you will come to the town of Llanberis, though there is not much to speak of it other than to say that many use it as a base camp for climbing Yr Wyddfa.

Beyond the town even the Glyders fade to nothing and the landscape becomes rolling, full of sheep farms and villages with names like Bryngwyn and Plas Tirion. It is a pastoral landscape until you come to Caernarfon, which I have always found to be a queer sort of place myself. Many have praised the castle but having spent my entire life at Cythry it is, to myself, nothing. The town is beyond its prime. It is superfluous to the needs of modern society as there is nothing of any significance, barring the castle and gaol, for its size. It has no industry of which speak and it is hardly considered as a place for trade. It serves little purpose and I can well see a time when all that remains here are the ruins of the castle.

It does, however, sit upon our western boundary, the Menai, or Y Sain Cerddoriaeth. The strait is a bugger but one cannot help but love it dearly. Lord Nelson called it the most dangerous stretch of water surrounding the British Isles and I'll be damned if he wasn't right. Ships and sailors have always, since the Welsh first took to water, fallen victim to its eddies and whirlpools and so shall it always be until the day of judgement is at hand. There is even a statue to that great man on the banks of the Menai, though sadly on the side of Mon where it can not be claimed as a feature of Morfasson country. It is inscribed with the words 'ENGLAND EXPECTS THAT EVERY MAN WILL DO HIS DUTY.' Considering that it is located in Wales and as far as you can get (barring the length of Mon) from the border with England I consider this to be a kick in the teeth towards us Welsh. It is as if it were purposely inscribed as a reminder of the conquest, a signifier that the Welsh are subservient to the English.

During the last century this dear bugger has twice been tamed. The first time was early in the century when Thomas Telford placed his beautiful suspension bridge here. It is, to be brief on the matter, a wonder of modern architecture. The second time this bugger was tamed with a bridge that is very much not a wonder. This is Mr Stephenson's box girder bridge and woe was the order of the day when he completed that monstrosity. Never in all my life and all my travels across the world have I seen such a despicable and unnatural structure.

The Cerddoriaeth may not be the prettiest stretch of water in the land, and if it had never formed somebody would surely have cut a canal where it now lies, but it does not deserve a blight such as that bridge across it.

At the northern end of the strait we come to perhaps the grandest and most eloquent, desirable settlement in the whole of Morfasson country, Bangor Ah, if my ancestors had the sense to build Cythry overlooking that place it could not be a more astounding city. It is the Vienna of Wales, a city of high learning, arts and culture. It may not have the same architectural merits as that Austrian city but it has many of the same erudite qualities. Ecclesiastics have always been a part of life here. The city was built around the cathedral, founded by Deiniol in 525, and men have always come here to learn and debate ecumenical matters. In recent years there has been founded there a wondrous institution, the University College of North Wales, and it deserves to be ranked amongst the finest in the world, amongst the Yales and the Harvards. Perhaps one day it will surpass even Oxford and Cambridge as the premier seat of learning in Great Britain. Scholars flock there from all over the land and though they go in as boys they come out as men who shall accomplish astonishing feats and who shall change the world as we know it.

Bangor is also, thanks again to the cathedral, a seat of the most civilized arts and culture. In the medieval period the bards came here to serenade the bishops of Bangor and although many of their songs and sonnets have been lost their praise drew ever more of their contemporaries and until the Edwardian conquest Bangor was called 'the Bardic city.' Their influence remains and across the centuries

Bangor has produced a wealth of composers, opera stars and music hall entertainers. Betws may have cornered the market in artists but Bangor can certainly claim the remainder of the cultural pantheon. Many is the night, for example, I have drifted into fantasy whilst seated in my favourite place at the opera house.

Each city and town of a region is a part of its soul and Bangor is the beating heart of Morfasson country. It is the most lively and vibrant settlement and no other west of the Conwy can compare. But, alas, Bangor is a pure heart. Its ecclesiastical history has made it a virtuous place and has left the door open for elsewhere to seize the vices that shroud the darker side of vibrant settlements. In our region those vices have been taken up by Bethesda, which lies at the head of Dyffryn Ogwen, sandwiched neatly between the Glyderau and Carneddau. Although its predominant industry is the mining of slate it has also developed a promiscuous sideline over the previous fifty years. The seedy devils of society are drawn to the place, the same kind who wish for things that are frowned upon by civilized folk. Until the death of Victoria Bethesda's vice of choice was opium whilst prostitution and gambling were minor players. Since, and thanks to the decline of the opium trade, the prostitution industry has been in the ascendancy.

Gambling has also grown and is a fairly large part at the present time although I have noticed that the authorities, the police and the like, are currently taking an unusually keen interest in the underground dens and illicit casinos. I suspect the hand of the Penrhyns in this as gambling is one of their principle bug bears. When I was young boy I stumbled upon a cock fight after hustling my way into one of the bars. I bet a two guinea piece my father had given me and I was elated when I doubled my money. I placed half my winnings on a second fight but lost them when a militia, headed by the then Lord Penrhyn, as he was known, stormed the place and I found myself with all the other gamblers in a cell of Caernarfon Gaol. Lord Penrhyn recognized me but he still insisted I be taken away with the others. In his opinion anybody who gambled, no matter who they were, ought to be punished with the utmost severity.

The Barons Penrhyn are the principle aristocratic family of the region. In fact, today there are no others. They own a large proportion of land in the region, half of the respectable side of Bethesda, and yet they couldn't care a jot for the place. To my eyes all they appear interested in is desecrating the mountainsides in the search for wealth, and exploiting a people who have little choice but to work for them. It is small wonder that living under their yolk, as many Bethesdans do, has caused people to turn to prostitution and opium and gambling.

The remainder of the region's wealthy are a more wholesome people. There is no one place where you find them collected, though there are large concentrations in the area around Bangor's opera house and in Conwy. These are people who, unlike the Penrhyns, actually care for the land and who actually want to live here rather than spending a few weeks out of every summer locked inside a ridiculously ostentatious folly. They, as all the native peoples of the region with the exception of the Frodorion, are jolly and friendly and welcoming. They are also forthright in their opinions and they will ensure that you know what they think. They will never argue with you but they will always be happy to debate so long as the drink is flowing and the sun has not yet risen. They have their gripes but for the most part they are a contented people. Be warned however, if ever you wrong them you will be sure to know of it. They take justice seriously in this part of the world and so long as it can be dealt in some way then it shall surely be done in a prompt fashion.

I cannot leave off this overview of my homeland without mentioning its principle attractions, the ranges of the Glyderau and Carneddau. Although they are only separated by the thin strip of Dyffryn Ogwen they could not be more different. The Glyder range is narrow with all its peaks arranged, more or less, in a row along the side of the valley. Its peaks are pointy and rugged and when the clouds are grey and low they look truly mystical. Of its delights you will discover Llyn Idwal, surrounded by a rocky amphitheatre known as 'The Devil's Kitchen' and fed, when there has not been a considerable dearth of rain at least, by a cascade known as 'The Devil's Appendix.' All of the Glyder peaks are memorable but the one that is the most memorable of all is Tryfan. It may not be large but its hump backed, dragon like appearance has never been forgotten by any who have set eyes upon it. It is one of two peaks in the Glyderau, the other being Elidir Fawr, to stand apart from the main ridge. But whereas Elidir fawr has been irreparably damaged by the quarrymen Tryfan remains whole. Legends surround this range, legends of Arthur and of reclusive, fur covered ape men but I shall not go into those for the moment.

On the opposing side of Dyffryn Ogwen are the Carneddau. The Ogwen edge of this range, due to long ago glaciation, is just as sharp and just as rugged as its opposing counterpart but rise above the level of the valley and the mountains begin to roll, the peaks blending together into one contiguous mass with little to separate them but shallow, grassy dips and the occasional wide valley towards the peripheries. The peaks themselves are not sharp, like the Glyders, but rotund, mostly indistinguishable from one another. There is but one truly sharp mountain, Yr Elen, and like Tryfan it resembles a sleeping dragon, albeit one who has been far more worn down by the ages. As I say, it is the sharpest of the Carneddau but not so sharp as any of the Glyders. The range rolls down towards the sea and then narrows into a thin wedge that culminates at Conwy with the minor gnoll of Mynydd Y Dref.

Detractors say that the Carneddau are without spectacle and that they are dull but I would disagree, and not solely because they are my home range. These rolling gnolls form a high plain that is unrivalled by any other landscape in the British Isles. You can feel truly alone up there and you will almost never see another living soul. And the lakes are beautiful too. Often set down from the high peaks in their own enclosure there are no fewer than ten of them, not counting Llyn Ogwen or some of the smaller tarns you find thereabout. What I say is that whilst the Carneddau may not have the crags and crevices of the Glyderau they are just as beautiful and equally as spectacular in their own special way.

Morfasson country is a varied land, a land that includes mountain ranges, forests of mystery and places that will haunt your dreams forever. It is a land of wilderness and of civilization, where high culture and vice are but five miles distant and both rub shoulders with supreme isolation. There is a saying in this part of the world: Paradise is a myth, but what we have here is as near as anyone will ever get.

THE COFFEE HOUSE INTERVIEWS

Anna: A Lady of Class

She knows how to make an entrance; barging through the door of the coffee house ten minutes late and flinging her overcoat at a leaving customer, fully expecting them to suddenly become her personal cloak room attendant. She then sits at a different table to the one that I am on, one closer to the window, and starts clicking her fingers at the barista behind the counter.

'You, girl,' she shouts loud enough that the whole house can hear. 'I shall have a black tea with lemon. Quick sharp if you wouldn't mind.' The barista is so frightened that she gets to it at once. I have to admit that I'm scared as well, though that doesn't stop me getting up and moving over to Anna's table. If this scenario proves anything, it's that when Anna is around things will be her way or not at all. If she thinks something improper it will go out of the proverbial window.

'I only agreed to meet you here because Max convinced me,' she huffs. 'This is an awful place.' She looks around and sneers at the décor. 'What is wrong with a refined dining establishment?' A refined dining establishment, I point out, is not a good place for an informal interview. Business meetings perhaps, but not a chat. 'Nonsense! Alice and I meet with Lady Beddgelert in the *Albion Dining Rooms* every week. That is the classiest establishment in Bangor and it is ideal for our gossips.' This is not gossip though, I tell her. 'Well. Even more reason for us not to be here. If this is not gossip then we have no excuse not to have met in the Albion.'

Anna loves to gossip and as her tea arrives, the barista trembling, she begins telling me the latest news from high society (the latest news from 1920, of course.)

'Lady Prestatyn has been poisoning her husband,' she whispers. She doesn't say this as though it is rumour but outright fact. 'She told The Duchess of St Helens that she's been buying arsenic to get rid of the weeds in her garden.' And that's unusual for 1920? 'She doesn't have a garden! She lives in a Mayfair townhouse! So what is she doing with the arsenic? If it were for rats I might understand, but then why say she is getting rid of weeds?' Anna picks up her tea and sniffs it as though Lady Prestatyn has dropped arsenic into it. Drinking it, she purses her lips in disapproval but does not comment.

From the moment she steps into your life you can tell that Anna is a sophisticated lady. She wears her regality on her sleeve, in the way she walks, in the way she talks, in the way she behaves. This is understandable given that there was a time in her life when she *was* a step above us all on the social ladder. She was a princess.

'I still might have been one if it weren't for those god awful men.' She is referring to the leaders of a revolution in her kingdom of Ardeluta, now part of Romania, some forty years ago (from her perspective). 'It was absolutely terrible. Carlo (her brother and heir to the kingdom) struck a peasant farmer for insubordination and then things flared up and we had to run away. Of course, he shouldn't have done it, hit the peasant I mean, but it was still an overreaction to depose us.'

Things were not that simple though. The revolution was the end result of years of high taxation and oppression by the ruling family, the striking of the peasant being the final straw. 'The oppression was hardly our fault. It was the people who came before us. Father did his best to relieve the situation, to lower taxes, but it wasn't good enough. And how were we to know there was an international anarchist group operating under our noses?'

The silver lining, after being chased across Europe, was that she found herself under the protection of the man who was to change her life, Max Morfasson.

'I thought he was very impudent and rude when we first met. He was very controlling, wishing me to do all this and that. He claims it was for my own protection and he has a point but some of it, like making me ride in a third class choo-choo carriage, was completely uncalled for. I foiled him on that one of course. I *had* to. I couldn't spend the night with the low born women we were sharing a compartment with. They were ghastly. So I upgraded our tickets when he wasn't looking.'

Less than a week later Max and Anna were married.

'I loved him by then, of course I did, how could I not? But we were manipulated by the local hill farmers. We had not even admitted our love to ourselves, let alone each other, but they convinced us both that we were destined to be lovers and that we ought to get married right away. Absolute hokum!'

Was it though? Max and Anna are still together forty years later and she herself just said she loves him.

'Oh, it wasn't hokum that we were in love. That much was true. But we needn't have got married there and then. And the way they suggested it… All through dreams and prophecies and such nonsense. I didn't believe in things like that then and I certainly don't believe in them now.' So why, if she didn't believe in those things, did she go through with it? Instead of giving an answer she looks me over with a withering glare. I don't ask again but instead wonder what Max thinks of what happened 'Max is a gullible imbecile when it comes to such things. He believes in fairies and ghosts and all kinds of nonsense. He thinks the farmers were absolutely right.'

The form and suddenness of the marriage, which was a traditional hill farmer's ceremony, caused a scandal amongst the upper classes.

'Everybody thought we'd been through some pagan ritual. We hadn't, it was perfectly Christian, but because we hadn't married in church it wasn't seen as proper. It was legal, they had to admit as much, but it wasn't proper. When the news broke we had the late Marquess of Anglesey banging on the front door calling us heathens and a disgrace to society. That was very hypocritical of him considering he used to go around in women's clothing and ended up having his marriage annulled. The Beddgelerts understood though they were still shocked by the suddenness of it.'

Despite being a former princess and a well-known figure in high society, her best friend is the Dowager Lady Beddgelert, wife of the last Earl who fell from a precipice in 1886, Anna has no titles of merit. She is a simple Mrs. No longer a princess thanks to the dissolution of her kingdom, and not a countess or a lady or anything of any rank.

'I have grown used to it. The idea of being Lady Morfasson appeals to me but Max is unlikely to be given a peerage. As a foreigner they certainly won't give *me* one. I doubt that Max will be knighted either, despite all he's done for his country.'

She begins to go off on a tangent.

'You know, when the national intelligence services were set up around ten years ago nobody informed us or asked for advice or anything. We only found out from Sir David Windrush, who was in the civil service at the time. He died last year. Max is the foremost expert in espionage in the country, and probably the most experienced spy too. And nobody thought to consult him.' Is she forgetting Sidney Reilly, the so called 'Ace of Spies?' Is he not more expert in espionage than Max? 'No he is not. How old is Reilly? Max has at least twenty years on him and he's been doing it all since he was born. I doubt the same could be said of Reilly. He's not a nice man either. There is something sinister about him. You'd think that would be true of all spies, considering that it is a sinister profession, but I've spent enough time working with Max to know that it isn't. Most of them are perfectly amiable and polite. Some are even charming. In that line of work you have to leave everything at the office door. If you don't then you're in trouble.'

Does she, I wonder, find it difficult to keep certain things to herself, certain matters of espionage that she is inevitably privy too?

'Max is constantly telling me not to gossip about some things but I always tell Lady Beddgelert, whatever it might be. I can trust her and she has not once betrayed my confidence. She knows that our work is very important.'

Coming up fast, Anna knows, is the next generation. Her only son, Monty, recently returned from a three year spell in

India and is currently engaged to Alice, eldest daughter of Count Nuneaton.

'Montgomery is slowly taking over the family business and he's bringing Alice into things as his partner. He isn't there yet, but he'll cope given enough time. Max is not as young as he was. He's seventy five now and he can't keep working for much longer. I thought last year that might be it, that I might lose him. He developed a fever and he was bedridden for three weeks. Monty was still in India and I had to call him back at once. Max recovered, thank goodness.' She begins to grumble and diverts again. 'The India business was a silly thing though. I should never have had to call Montgomery back. He got this notion in his head that he wanted to go to France and fight in the war. When that was ruled out of the question he decided to pursue Alice to India instead. Then… And this is the silliest thing of all… He gets himself caught up in some nasty business on the North West Frontier. He's lucky to be alive, foolish boy.' What does she think of Alice, her future daughter in law? 'She is a good girl, though sometimes too flippant for my tastes. Montgomery loves her. That is what matters.'

Anna, overall, seems content with the hand that life has

drawn her but is this even close to what she imagined when she was young?

'No. Do not be so foolish. Which of us ever gets what we imagined when we were young? I certainly never thought that I would get married, especially not in a traditional hill farmer's ceremony. If I did get married I thought it would be to someone of Father's choosing. A Viennese whirl instead of a Welsh dumpling. I think I much prefer my life the way it turned out to how I imagined it would be. As nice as a Viennese whirl is, it isn't very filling. I'd rather have my Welsh dumpling.'

There is something of the Lady Bracknell about Anna, something high class, waspish and snobbish. But she doesn't just command the respect and admiration of those around her, nor does she demand it. She sucks it in like a human vacuum cleaner. Respect for her is the natural order of the universe. Throughout our interview all eyes have been turned towards her, everybody listening to what she has to say. It is no wonder, when she arrived on these shores forty years ago, that Max and the people of his small corner of Wales, fell in love with her. Everybody in this coffee house has just done the same. You just can't help it.

Max: The Spy Master

The Max who greets me with a wide smile and an eccentric handshake is not the Max of yesteryear, not the svelte, athletic, Victorian gentleman who once rode the mountain wildernesses with a Romanian princess at his side. That Max is still there, somewhere, but today he's been redecorated as a late Edwardian, is plump around the middle, and there's a tiredness to his eyes. Mind you, it's not surprising. He isn't young any more. By the standards of the times he is an old man.

'I ought to be retired,' he complains. 'I'll be seventy six next year. Nearly all other men of my class and age have put their feet up, gone into collecting butterflies or stuffed animals…' A defiant twinkle enters his eye. 'Still, I suppose if I were a casual labourer I might still be hard at it. Most people don't get the luxury of sitting down and collecting butterflies.' Does his wife, Anna, want him to retire? 'Of course, *she* wants to me to retire… She's wanted me to retire for twenty years. I doubt she'd let me collect butterflies though. Stuffed animals are well out of the question!'

To return to the beginning, Max was born in a wildly

different time, 1845, the son of Albert and Lavinia Morfasson.

'And then came Mable when I was around… Around five I think it was,' he smiles. 'Mother and Father, lovely people. They were kind and generous and ever so lovely. Not an ounce of cruelty in them. But Mable… Ahhh… She was a different kettle. I'm often convinced that she was a succubus, implanted in my mother by the devil, disguised as my father in the way old Jove used to do it in the mythologies. She was such a horrible little squit.' I beg him to expand further, though he is reluctant to talk. 'That is all gone now… All in the past. She walked out shortly after Father died, broke Mother's already bleeding heart. I haven't seen her since, though she wrote to Mother once. Mother burned the letter without reading it.' Does Max think she'll ever come back? 'I doubt it. It's been fifty years since she was last heard from and I doubt there would be any reason for her to return now. No. She's gone forever.'

I ask him about his parents, Albert and Lavinia, and he becomes more cheery, a boyish grin emerging from beneath his greying beard.

'Father sometimes came across as a very forthright man,

very hard working, very stiff... He was of that age. Sentiment was an alien concept to his generation. It was on the surface anyway. I remember, once, Nanny and I came in from our walk to find him sat on the floor of the nursery playing with my toy soldiers. Denied it of course, said he was only looking at them, but he was definitely playing. As I said before, he was never cruel. Never once. He abhorred unnecessary violence, preferred to deal in words where he could. He passed that on to me and I have *tried* to pass it on myself, though I'm afraid I haven't had much luck there.'

What about Lavinia?

'Mother? Oh, she was very playful, very sweet. She was quite at odds with the Welsh mountains, much preferred our summer residence in Yorkshire... But she taught me a lot about horses and how to ride. She had me riding about the mountains on my own by the time I was five. Mother loved horses but I suppose anybody would if their father owned fifteen stud farms.'

Whilst Max was studying in Dublin, at age nineteen, his father suffered a catastrophic stroke. He was required to abandon his studies and to immediately take over the family business.

'Mother was a fantastic help in all that. I was keen on studying law, thought it might help when it came to running the business, but when Father suffered his stroke I had to give all that up. I've been grateful for it in these later years though. Mother taught me a lot and Father was a great help too, when he started to recover a little. I wouldn't have got that if I continued my studies. I've tried things a little different with Monty. I thought, if anything were to happen suddenly he'd be better off if I had taught him dribs and drabs from a young age, built him up. Then he went running off to India in pursuit of a girl and all my plans went to rot.'

This, during the First World War, was a particular low point for Max. Monty went behind his and Anna's back and signed up to fight in France. The pair were livid, Max especially so.

'Anna and I tried for years to conceive him. We'd practically given up by the time he did come along. Then he decides he wants to throw his life on the western front!' Max's eyes darken. He looks grim. 'That war... What the devil was it? It was some bloody minded squabble between politicians, orchestrated by a closeted, fantasy dwelling elite. How many times does a brigade have to be cut down by machine gun fire before the generals realise that walking directly into it isn't going to work? I am actually quite glad that I managed to get Monty out of that one. Yes, he ended up in India instead and there was a bit of a hoo-hah out there, but it turned out alright in the end. Pity the same can't be said about the girl!' Max rolls his eyes. He does not approve, I presume? 'It isn't that I don't approve of the match. She's a pleasant girl. I do like her... But her family,' by which he means the Fletchers of Nuneaton, "are another matter entirely. Count Fletcher was jailed for fraud and defamation a couple of years ago. His wife ought to have got the same but she ran away to the continent and took a lover, or so my wife tells me. I don't like the family at all. They're trouble.'

He clearly does not want to talk about *them* so I push Max onto another topic, the spying game, that which he has dedicated his life to. In his early years he had his pick of the crop, lucrative contracts and a genial relationship with the British government, despite Queen Victoria's dislike of the family.

'We never got anything from Victoria," Max explains. "She held a grudge because Father refused to dedicate a memorial to Prince Albert. Edward VII was the same as his mother, though George has been a bit more genial. Mostly we got things direct from whoever was in charge. Liberal governments were always giving us things but in Tory times we could go months without a contract. We had other things to keep us busy though.'

Max is overcome by a rage. It is not often he becomes angry but this, which he is about to enter into, is one of the topics which sets him off. In 1909 the British Government founded the Secret Service Bureau, later to become MI5 and 6, and Max was pushed out into the cold.

'It was like we didn't matter. It was a brutal kicking, especially from a government which we'd had dealings with only the year before. We weren't even consulted, weren't asked for advice or assistance or anything. I know the game better than anybody who was a part of that whatever they called it. I've been doing it all my life. You'd have thought that somebody might have given me a cursory nod.' Was the SSB not, I question, set up because of the threat posed by the German Empire? Was it not founded on a need to have a continuously operating force rather than relying on a mercenary agency? 'Yes… That I have no problem with, though I'm sure the threat from Germany was exaggerated, at least it was to some extent. What annoys me is that we were ignored, pushed aside. They went behind our backs. After that thing was set up we got *nothing* from the government for years. Monty did some work for them out in India and since then they've been a bit more genial, but it isn't what it was.' Max looks glum, morose, out of sorts. He is clearly still upset by the snub, even all these years later.

As well as witnessing the formation of the SSB, Max has also lived through increasingly turbulent times. He was born at the height of the British Empire, during a time of relative peace, but in his lifetime the world has become ever more violent and volatile.

'I don't like it,' Max admits. 'I saw the last war coming with all the anti-German bollocks that was being stirred up by the likes of Northcliffe, but nobody in charge seems to have learned anything. The aristocrats are still going around as though nothing has changed. They're still as empty headed as they ever were, especially the ones who are coming through now, the ones who weren't old enough to fight in the war. There are bleak times ahead. The next generation might not see the end of them, and nor might the one after or the one after them."

I see he is worried for the future, for the twentieth century. Dare I tell him of what is to come? Of the Second World War and the rise of fascism, of what is to come after with the Cold War, of the increasingly turbulent situation in the Middle East? Dare I tell him of the chain reaction ignited by the first war and of the events which he himself has lived through? I don't think I need to for I sense that he already knows the answers. Though he will not live to see it, the future terrifies him.

"What happened to the world? What happened to the people in it? Things never used to be perfect but there was always polity and morality and respect. There was never all this extreme xenophobia that's been going around these last twenty years. There was never all this selfish cruelty towards other people. There certainly wasn't this same tendency for bloody minded incompetence.'

And what of his family, of the future of his dynasty? Does he ever wonder if that is in safe hands?

'It is for the immediate future. Monty shall be a fair enough head for the business. He'll get the job done. After that I couldn't possibly comment. It depends on the times and what Monty's children get up to. If the Fletchers are anything to go by, and there is some especially bad blood in that family, those children could prove our undoing…' He raises an ominous eyebrow. 'Then again, I have the strongest conviction that so long as Monty is around those children won't be allowed to put a single toe out of line.' Max looks into his cup and realises that his coffee is finished. He puffs himself up and readjusts the buttons on his waistcoat. 'Whatever the future brings, we'll face it. We'll muddle through, bad blood or no. We Morfas have survived the worst this world can throw at us and we'll survive a lot more before it all comes crushing down!'

He has no idea how right he is.

THE FURTHER ADVENTURES OF THE MORFAS FAMILY

In the years since Max wrote his memoires volume my family, the Fabanau-Morfa (that's the plural by the way) have had some astonishing adventures. Many of these involve our continuing battles against the nefarious SHEMBLE but others cover our involvement in the great events of the last century; the First World War, the Punk revolution, the swinging sixties and so on.

With the help of my brother James (adopted) and his astonishing literary talents, we are bringing these tales to the public through a fusion of new and original texts, such as the one you have just read. If you have enjoyed this volume then I am sure you will be excited to continue to voyage down our little rabbit hole in the years to come. I look forwards to one day welcoming you back with open arms.

-Marco Morfa

WHERE TO NEXT?

You've read about how our long feud with SHEMBLE began, but now dear reader two paths lie before you, twisting and intersecting. Sometimes distinct, sometimes not. So which path will you tread?

The story of our duel against SHEMBLE continues in ***Charlie Fuller***- A boy, obsessed with growing a moustache, makes an enemy of his wicked headmaster, Augustus Carrion. Yet, when Charlie meets a dashing young gentleman he discovers that Carrion is an evil man, a man who is indoctrinating his best friend into his organisation: SHEMBLE.

To learn more of the infernal abyss, you should read: ***Red Bird***- Outed as gay and fearing persecution, Tom Lime flees to the city of Liverpool where he meets and falls in love with the charming Gwyn Geulan. But something strange is happening in Liverpool, and Lime must make a terrifying journey into the underworld to uncover the truth.

THE ANCIENT HOUSE OF MORFA

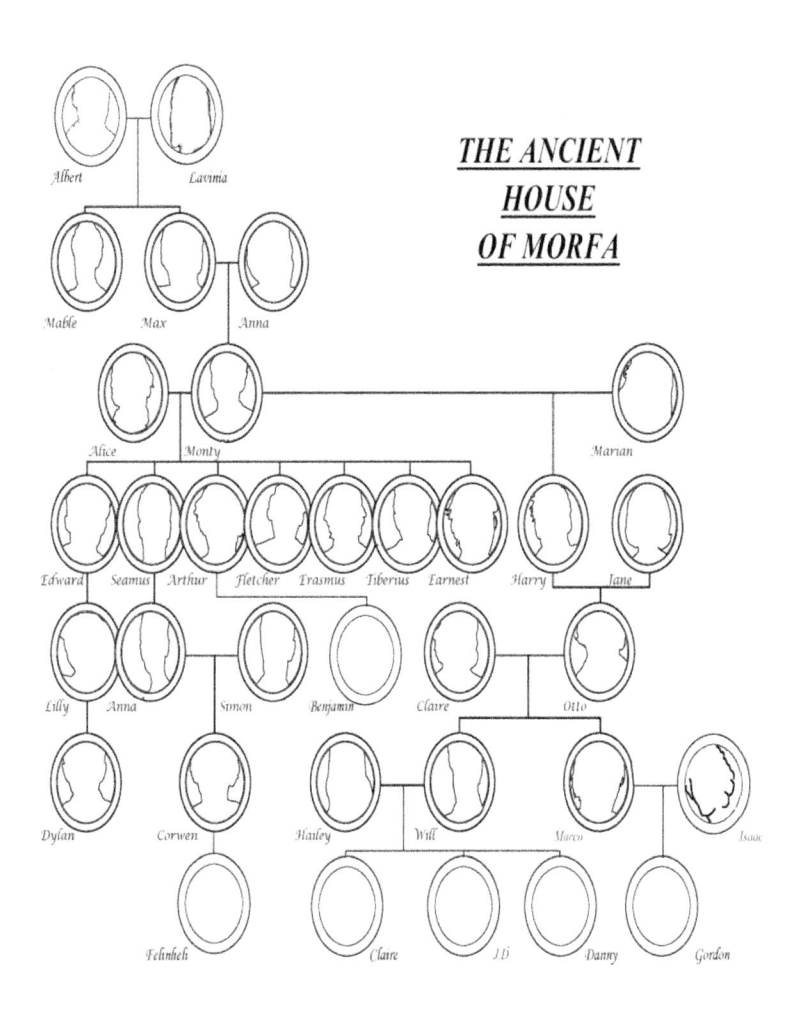

- Albert — Lavinia
  - Mable
  - Max
  - Anna — Alice / Monty — Marian
    - Edward
    - Seamus — Anna (Lilly)
      - Dylan
    - Arthur — Simon
      - Corwen
        - Felinheli
    - Fletcher
    - Erasmus
    - Tiberius
    - Earnest
    - Benjamin
    - Claire — Harry / Jane — Otto
      - Hailey — Will
        - Claire
        - JD
        - Danny
      - Marco — Isaac
        - Gordon

Printed in Great Britain
by Amazon